Alexander Golitsyn, the stolen NOC list safely stored in his inside breast pocket, quickly navigated through a throng of people.

Ethan checked his Visco monitor, and saw that Jim Phelps was at the other side of the bridge, peering over his shoulder through the rising fog. Suddenly, the barrel of a gun aimed point-blank at Jim became perfectly visible on Ethan's tiny screen. A static-filled pop burst from the microspeaker, and the transmission went momentarily crazy.

When the image resolved, there was a bloody hole in the center of Jim's chest.

Ethan heard sounds along the promenade. He ran toward the end of the bridge and saw Golitsyn walking briskly. Ethan started to give chase, glancing back at the transport vehicle, where he saw Claire's outline in the driver's seat. And in the instant while Ethan thought about what he was going to say to her, the car blew twenty feet into the air and turned into a rolling fireball.

"Claire!" Ethan screamed, covering up from raining glass and debris.

Ahead, Golitsyn finally slowed down, reaching some kind of marker or rendezvous point. He edged toward an archway and seemed to speak with another person hiding in the alley. Suddenly, Golitsyn straightened up, then crumpled to the ground. As Golitsyn's body fell, an arm reached from behind the archway and pulled something from Golitsyn's jacket.

Ethan burst out of the fog and moved to Golitsyn's body. Blood was soaking his clothes. A quick inspection of his pockets turned up nothing. Not a key, a coin, or even a piece of lint.

There was nothing else for Ethan to do. No transport. No backup. Ethan whirled around to see policemen charging through the fog.

It was time to run.

MISSION: IMPOSSIBLE

A NOVEL BY PETER BARSOCCHINI
STORY BY DAVID KOEPP AND STEVEN ZAILLIAN
SCREENPLAY BY DAVID KOEPP AND ROBERT TOWNE

POCKET BOOKS
New York   London   Toronto   Sydney   Tokyo   Singapore

This book is a work of fiction. Names, characters, places and incidents are products of the author's imagination or are used fictitiously. Any resemblance to actual events or locales or persons, living or dead, is entirely coincidental.

An *Original* Publication of POCKET BOOKS

POCKET BOOKS, a division of Simon & Schuster Inc.
1230 Avenue of the Americas, New York, NY 10020

ISBN: 0-671-54921-9

First Pocket Books printing June 1996

10 9 8 7 6 5 4 3 2 1

POCKET and colophon are registered trademarks of Simon & Schuster Inc.

Cover design by Bryan Allen, 5555 Communications

Printed in the U.S.A.

Part One

THE MOLEHUNT

Kiev

A STEELY COLD RAIN BEAT DOWN ON KIEV, DRAWING OIL out of the roadways and infusing the old city with an industrial smell. At 2 A.M. the streets were deserted, except for occasional cars splashing through puddles and squealing around corners, shattering the steady rhythm of the rain. The only people on the streets at this hour were either drunk or dangerous, most likely both.

A police car roared down a potholed street in the worst part of the city, its siren slashing the tense silence inside a tattered hotel room, where the bloodied corpse of a young woman was sprawled across a thin mattress. Blood was splattered on the dimly lit room's faded red velvet curtains and stained the worn wooden floor. Whoever murdered this girl acted in rage, and wasn't worried about leaving a mess.

Gennady Kasimov, a disheveled-looking man with

3

a gray, fleshy face, sat in the room that reeked of cigarettes and stale steam heat, his head rocking back and forth in groggy disbelief. The pulsing whine of the police car's siren snapped Kasimov to attention, and revealed animal fear in his milky green eyes. When the police car sped past the hotel, Kasimov felt little comfort because he knew this hotel was a location where vice officers often visited three or four times a night. The next car might stop, looking for him.

Kasimov breathed heavily. His head throbbed and every time he moved he felt nauseous. Making it infinitely worse for him was the dead woman lying on the bed.

He stared at her, confused and frightened. A single bare lightbulb dangled from the ceiling cord, bathing the young woman's bloody body in an unforgiving flat pallor. How did this happen? Kasimov labored to piece together the events of the night. He had gone to a private bar, a place reserved for government officials and wealthy businessmen. It was the same bar he had been going to for years, except now he drank there for free because, in the newly democratized Russia, Kasimov was an up-and-coming politician who could do people favors. Everyone wanted to buy him drinks, slap his back, and put envelopes in his jacket to ensure the wheels of government kept turning in their favor. Plenty of drinks had already gone down when he met this girl, an absolute beauty who liked to drink and dance and couldn't take her eyes, or hands, off him. Kasimov, knowing he was far from Kiev's most handsome man, assumed the girl wanted something—a favor, a job, perhaps a word passed upstairs on behalf of a family member. Everybody wanted something. So why not enjoy this beauty? Maybe he would do the favor for her, maybe he wouldn't, depending on how convincingly she made the request.

So he left with her for another bar, drank some more, then stumbled into a taxi with her.

That was the last thing he remembered.

Now he found himself in this firetrap Kiev whorehouse, still dressed in his wrinkled blue suit, bloodstains on his sleeves and congealed blood on his fingers.

As the siren of the police car faded in the distance, Kasimov breathed deeply, then looked up at a burly, pockmarked, middle-aged man named Anatoly Cherenovsky, who paced slowly around the room. Cherenovsky was a Russian crime boss whom Kasimov had seen in person only once before, but knew to be someone who solved insoluble problems. Mobsters had always controlled Russia's black market, but in this new era of capitalism and democracy, they also controlled most of Russia's burgeoning businesses and half of the government. Kasimov hoped and prayed that Cherenovsky would save him from this nightmare.

"I don't remember this, I don't remember what happened," Kasimov vowed to Cherenovsky, his voice raw and shaky.

"Of course you don't remember," Cherenovsky answered, glancing at the woman's body. "Why would you want to remember such a horrible event?" His tone was businesslike but suspicious. This was not the first time Cherenovsky had seen a dead woman next to a man who conveniently remembered nothing.

"No, no, I swear," Kasimov insisted, "we were at

the bar, drinking, laughing, having fun. She liked me. She liked me very much."

Cherenovsky raised one of the woman's eyelids, revealing a glassy stare; she'd been dead at least an hour.

"I think she liked you better earlier in the evening," Cherenovsky observed. "But I see the attraction. Very pretty." Kasimov circled the bed, then came to rest, his hand leaning on a closet door on the right side of the small room.

Inside the closet, a video monitor displayed the grim murder scene in stark black-and-white. The dead woman's blood looked like ink on the small monitor. Jack Kiefer, perched on a stool in this closet clogged with electronic devices, held his breath while he studied the screen intently. Kiefer was in his early thirties, with shaggy brown hair and the pale skin of someone unfamiliar with daylight; his shoulders were slumped from years spent at computer terminals, his eyes edgy and alert. As Kasimov took his hand off the door, Kiefer silently let his breath out in relief. But his relief was short-lived.

"She's been under too long," he said nervously to himself, staring at the corpse.

Kasimov wiped blood off his fingers and covered his face with his hands. "I don't even know how I got here. Anatoly, I did not touch her. I didn't do this!"

Anatoly Cherenovsky leaned down and looked carefully at the girl.

"Ah, I know this girl," he said quietly.

Kasimov's mouth dropped open but he couldn't get a sound out. It could be only bad news for Kasimov that Cherenovsky recognized the girl.

"She is one of Vladensky's girls. One of his favorites. This was not a good choice, Kasimov. Did you have to pick such a beautiful girl?"

"God," Kasimov muttered, realizing the enormity of his situation. "My God . . ." Vladensky was another crime boss, even more powerful than Cherenovsky.

"Don't weep like a child," Cherenovsky said to Kasimov.

Kasimov wiped the sweat out of his eyes and tried to stop trembling. He had somehow killed the girlfriend of one of Russia's most feared gangsters, and though his brain was muddled he had enough clarity of mind to know that his life was suddenly worthless. Unless Anatoly Cherenovsky could help him.

"It's good you called me first," Cherenovsky said. "It's the only smart thing you've done tonight."

Back in the closet, Jack Kiefer piston-chewed a stick of gum and glanced at the screen of a laptop computer, which displayed a readout of human vital signs: blood pressure and heart rate were dropping, as was body temperature.

"This is taking too much time," he whispered to himself.

In the room, Kasimov wept. The minor Russian politician was falling apart, and he still hadn't given up the name that Cherenovsky demanded in return for helping him. Cherenovsky wanted the identity of one of Kasimov's contacts, a man known to be trading in espionage secrets. But Kasimov, even in his distress, was being tight-lipped on that subject.

"You're the only one who can help me," he said,

pleading with Anatoly Cherenovsky, reaching like a supplicant for one of his sleeves.

"Don't flounder," Cherenovsky said derisively, slapping Kasimov's hand away.

"But I need—"

Cherenovsky slapped Kasimov hard across the face.

"Tell me what I want to know," he said, anger rising in his voice. "My help doesn't come free. You knew that when you called me."

"They'll kill me," Kasimov said, shaking his head.

"And Vladensky will kill you if I don't help you. You asked for my help, Kasimov. Now talk to me." Cherenovsky slapped him again.

Out of respect and fear, Kasimov took the beating. But he did not talk.

Cherenovsky started for the door. "I've wasted enough time. I leave you to explain to Vladensky what happened to his girl."

Jack Kiefer nearly fell off his stool in the closet. "Don't walk out that door," he begged under his breath. "Please don't. We don't have time for that."

But Cherenovsky was already turning the door handle.

Kiefer checked the "dead" woman's vital signs on his computer screen. The woman was approaching the danger zone. For real.

Back in the room Kasimov pleaded. "Please! Please! Anatoly, please!"

Cherenovsky turned and stalked back toward Kasimov.

"The name," Cherenovsky demanded.

8

Kasimov wept and looked desperately at the dead girl.

"The name," Jack Kiefer repeated in his closet, "just give us the damn name."

"My contact is in Minsk," Kasimov blurted. "He works in a travel agency. That's all I know."

It wasn't enough.

"The name," Cherenovsky persisted. Tears and sweat rolled down Kasimov's face. "The *NAME!*" Cherenovsky finally screamed, inches away from Kasimov's face.

Kasimov buried his face in his arms. "His name is . . . Dimitri Miediev," he said, feeling the life drain from his own body. He clenched his hands into fists and beat himself on the head.

"Dimitri Miediev," Anatoly Cherenovsky repeated.

Inside the closet Jack Kiefer typed into his keyboard:

**MINSK/TRAVEL
AGENCY/MIEDIEV, DIMITRI**

The response came moments later:

posting/American consulate/Kiev

"Got him," Jack Kiefer said.

A whorehouse waitress swept into the room, carrying a tray with a bottle of premium vodka and two shotglasses.

"All will be well," Cherenovsky said to Kasimov, pouring out two shots, and shoving one to the trembling man. "I'll see to it."

"Yes, Anatoly, thanks to you, all will be well," Kasimov answered shakily, downing the shot.

Cherenovsky faced the closet and said, "Cheers."

He did not drink.

Vodka drooled down Kasimov's chin. His eyes rolled back into his head and he crashed to the floor.

Cherenovsky made no move to break his fall.

Instead, he ran to the closet and jerked it open, pulling at his chin with the other hand. The chin stretched out like bubble gum, and suddenly the pockmarked, rugged face of Anatoly Cherenovsky was vanishing into strips of Mylopar—the latest advance in synthetic skin developed in CIA labs—and latex that peeled away in layers to reveal the face of Ethan Hunt, a man in his early thirties with short black hair and the taut features of a well-conditioned athlete. He ripped off the straggling pieces of the Mylopar and latex base, which clung to his neck and forehead, pulled padding out of his jacket, and stripped a thin plastic overlay from his mouth that had given his teeth a yellowish tinge.

All around him, walls slid back, and the ceiling of the hotel room was lifted and lowered away, revealing a warehouse that surrounded the fake room. A team of men wearing dark green jumpsuits, working in precisely choreographed steps, executed the cleanup. The speed and efficiency displayed by the crew indicated they had done similar work many times before, and indeed they had, since this was an Impossible Mission Force team, here under the command of Ethan Hunt.

In fact, the only person in the entire warehouse not

part of the IMF team was Gennady Kasimov, the object of this sting.

Ethan Hunt snatched a small plastic box out of Jack Kiefer's hands and rushed over to the bed.

"Get that scum out of here," he snapped, stepping over Kasimov's body.

Instantly, two crew members dragged Kasimov away.

Ethan knelt over the woman on the bed, intense focus in his eyes.

"I don't know, Ethan," Jack Kiefer said, bursting out of his closet, looking uncertainly at the inert woman. "I don't trust this stuff. She was under way too long."

Ethan held up a hand, signaling Jack to stay back, while he opened the plastic kit, extracted a syringe, squirted a bit of fluid, then jammed the needle into her thigh. He gently picked up the woman's wrist and felt for a pulse.

"Oh, man," Jack Kiefer said nervously, shaking his head, "this can't be good."

"I had thirty seconds to spare," Ethan said to Jack, without looking at him. Ethan's eyes didn't move from the woman's face.

"How do you know?" Jack asked, though he'd worked with Ethan Hunt long enough to know that the guy had a clock built into his brain that was as good as the one in Jack's computer. Still, Claire hadn't moved.

Ethan Hunt understood Jack's concern. The young woman on the bed, Claire, was not an ordinary agent. She was married to Jim Phelps, the IMF director.

With one hand, Ethan raised the back of Claire's head; with the other, he softly stroked her face, trying to rouse her.

"Claire," he whispered, "Claire."

Claire's body remained lifeless, limp. Ethan's face betrayed his emotions—they were too late, and he was to blame. But just as Ethan lowered her body back down on the bed, Claire stirred. Her eyelids fluttered, then opened.

"Hello, Claire," Ethan said, his face only a few inches from hers.

She managed a small smile, and for a few seconds the two of them looked like young lovers stealing a moment of privacy. A faint smile crossed Ethan's lips.

"Did we get it?" Claire weakly whispered.

"We got it," Ethan said. "Now, on your feet."

She tried to push herself up, but fell back on the mattress, awash in fake blood.

"I want to sleep," she mumbled with her French accent. She tried to shake the grogginess from her head, but couldn't. "Can I sleep here?"

Ethan gently lifted her shoulders. "Walk," he said, helping her to her feet. "Just walk a bit." He picked up a bottle of mineral water, and poured a small amount into her mouth.

She swallowed, then attempted to walk, but fell against Ethan, who tried to get her moving.

Ethan knew that Jack was watching him, and that others were, too. He knew that his care of Claire probably appeared to them to be overly tender, and to the exclusion of other tasks that needed to be done. But right then he didn't care. He was tired; he'd been

12

working nonstop for nine weeks, and his guard was down. Ethan wanted to know that Claire was all right, and he hoped the others would assume his care of Claire was out of deference to his boss and friend, Jim Phelps.

"I'm walking," Claire mumbled, not walking at all, but still being held up by Ethan.

"Talking's good, walking's better," Ethan answered.

Claire finally steadied herself enough to step around a wall and change into her travel clothes.

After she finished, Jack Kiefer brought her a plastic bag containing personal belongings, and Claire buckled on her watch, then slipped on the diamond wedding ring Jim Phelps had given her when they married two years ago.

Ethan watched the ring slide onto Claire's finger. It had been a surprise to Ethan, and to everyone else within the IMF group, when Phelps and Claire announced their marriage. IMF work was dangerous, transitory, and impersonal. Relationships between operatives was frowned upon, and had been the cause of more than a few agents being dismissed over the years. In fact, it was Jim Phelps who dismissed them. He wanted his operatives to follow orders, and if a change in orders during a mission meant one of the agents would suddenly be in a perilous situation, Phelps didn't want the chain of command questioned or interfered with due to personal emotions. It was a sensible policy that Ethan agreed with; at least until he, too, met Claire. Occasionally, IMF recruited married couples, when their established relationship might serve as an effective cover in certain situations. But, generally speaking, it was bad business for agents to be married.

That Jim Phelps married one of his own operatives signaled to some within IMF a change in his professional standards, and to others that Claire must be an extraordinary woman. Ethan Hunt believed the latter.

Like Ethan, Jim Phelps did not readily reveal his personal thoughts and emotions. And he had done a good job of hiding his relationship with Claire. When the marriage was announced, however, Ethan reacted with little surprise; he had worked several missions with Claire, and had thought often about how he might get to know her even better. His respect for Phelps and IMF had kept him from acting too quickly with her. Then, quite suddenly, she was married—to Ethan's mentor and best friend. At that point there was nothing for him to do but move on. And do his job.

Claire used a specially treated towelette to wipe fake blood from her face, and Ethan walked over to inspect her eyes. They were still cloudy from the drug.

"Don't look so worried," Claire said to him.

"If you're going to use that stuff again," he said to her, "it's not going to be on my watch."

"Hey," she replied, acknowledging his concern with a slight smile, "I'm still standing."

The two of them exchanged looks, then Ethan checked the activity in the warehouse.

"Is there any reason we're still here?!" he yelled to the cleanup detail.

Suddenly, the pace of work picked up.

"Listen, buddy, the good guys won," Jack Kiefer

said lightly to Ethan, patting him on the shoulder. "Take it easy."

But Ethan didn't return his smile. He was edgy, watching Claire walk, still unsteadily, toward one of the vans waiting on the loading dock.

Then, when the last of the workers was out the door, Ethan made a final inspection.

He walked over to a dim section of the now empty warehouse and picked up a small button from the floor which hadn't been there when they'd arrived.

Ethan, always meticulous to the last detail, did not want the slightest chance that a dropped or misplaced object would jeopardize his mission. He dropped the button into his pocket and headed for the vans, leaving the warehouse precisely as they'd found it, empty and cold.

Mr. Phelps

CLAIRE PHELPS, IN THE PHOTOGRAPH HELD BY HER HUS-
band as he flew to Prague, looked enigmatic, with her
long dark hair spilling over part of her face, high
cheekbones setting off hazel eyes, and the same faint,
secretive smile that she displayed for Ethan in Kiev. It
was not without anxiety that Jim Phelps looked at the
picture of his wife.

After all, they were often separated, since his position as director of the IMF kept him on the move to
many places other than cities where his wife happened to be working on a mission. He entrusted her
care to Ethan Hunt, his most skilled and valued
subordinate, but of course that only breathed more
life into the bond that Jim knew already existed
between his young wife and Ethan. His anxieties
about Claire were useless, Jim knew, because what
control did he have over her anyway? Claire was not a

woman who could be possessed, only borrowed; she was private and unpredictable, which was part of the excitement of being with her. Still, thinking of her, these transatlantic flights were becoming less and less tolerable to Jim Phelps.

There had been a time when Jim actually enjoyed flying. Boarding an airplane in Rio de Janeiro, en route to Bangkok, or flying by private jet from La Jolla to Morocco on one hour's notice, represented freedom from the confines of society. It meant being light, unbound by the strictures and structures of a normal life, no worries about refrigerators to fill, doors that needed fixing, or lawns that needed mowing. Jim had no family obligations because he had no family. Except, of course, for Claire, but she was a recent development.

Phelps had spent the better part of the past thirty years traveling. And since it was useful in his business to refrain from forming close personal ties, constant travel was a way of staying a few steps ahead of feeling that life was happening all around Jim Phelps, but he could never quite reach out and touch it. He studied life in all its forms: he copied, imitated, faked, manipulated, and sometimes took life. But that was all business. And lately during these endless flights, in the long stretches of night when everyone else on the plane slept, Phelps stayed awake and ruminated about the fact that, for the first time since adolescence, he wondered if he was missing out on real life entirely. The last thirty years had been lived in the shadows of other people's lives, running missions so secret and effective that only a handful of people in the world knew the ripples of history created by Phelps and the

17

IMF. Only a select few could know how good the IMF was at their work because any acknowledgment of the IMF's existence weakened its effectiveness. What a strange way to live, Phelps mused, to be like a constant shadow, floating over the earth in a ceaseless orbit.

While he thought and stared at the dark horizon over the Atlantic, Jim toyed with his wedding ring, given him by Claire two years ago. Phelps, as he closed in on sixty years of age, was tired of policy. He didn't have to explain himself to Claire. She seemed to know his moods before he was aware of them himself. She knew when to draw close, and when to back off. Claire could excite him with the simple touch of her finger to his face. And these things he did not want to let slip away, IMF agent or not. In fact, it was Claire's coming into his life that had brought about this new mood of reassessment. Until Claire, the days and months and years had started to run together for him. She brought him back to the moment, yet the sudden intensity of feeling she ignited in him, in an odd way, also embittered Jim Phelps. He had given over his life to the IMF and the CIA. No birthday, anniversary, or holiday ever stood between him and a mission. And because of this relentless dedication, Phelps was regarded in the clandestine circles of cold warriors as perhaps the most effective operative of the post–World War II period. He had seen the Berlin Wall come down and the Soviet Union collapse; his role in those historic events would never be recorded, but IMF's invisible imprint helped shape history.

And what had the world given him in return? Perhaps, he decided, the world had given him Claire.

Jim had met Claire in Paris nearly three years ago when he recruited her from Interpol to work an IMF sting against a Libyan arms dealer. During that mission she played, prophetically, the role of his wife. Jim was then masquerading as a Swiss money launderer. The mission lasted three weeks, during which time Claire spent every waking minute with Jim, and he began to fall in love with her. After the mission they went to Fiji to escape any fallout from the Libyans. And while in Fiji Jim discovered for the first time in decades, perhaps for the first time in his life, that he could enjoy the constant presence of another person. It was all cliché, he knew, the fact that he felt like a young man around her, that food tasted better and that he wanted to look at sunsets, but it was all true.

Claire seemed delighted by what happened between them, but not surprised; being Parisian, she possessed the peculiarly French sense of fatalism about matters of the heart. He asked her to marry him, in fact, during a flight from Tangiers to Belize, and she said yes in a tone that indicated she'd known about their impending marriage long before Phelps had popped the question.

The plane's intercom clicked quietly. "Ladies and gentlemen," came the navigator's voice, "the captain has leveled us off at thirty-eight thousand feet for cruising altitude. We have plenty of calm air up here, so it should be a smooth flight all the way to Prague. We are going to Prague, aren't we? I guess so. Why not? Let us know if . . ." Great, Jim thought, we've got a comedian for a navigator. Jim tuned out the rest of the navigator's speech. He'd heard the same speech fifty thousand times and could fly this plane himself if he had to. Hell, once he had landed a 747 during a mission in Paraguay.

A cheery flight attendant began making rounds in the first-class cabin, passing out extra pillows and blankets—most of the passengers were already sleeping—and handing out flight folders. When she reached Jim Phelps her demeanor remained light and cheery, but she looked him steadily in the eye in a way that told him what he needed to know.

"Would you like to watch a movie, Mr. Phelps?" she asked pleasantly.

"No, I prefer the theater," he said lightly, looking away, checking other faces in the cabin.

The attendant nodded. "Would you consider the cinema of the Ukraine?"

"Perhaps you'd choose one for me," Jim said.

She returned to the front of the cabin. Jim pulled a pack of Marlboros from his jacket, slipped out a cigarette, and tapped it absently on the armrest, all the while studying the moves of the flight attendant who was digging around in an unlocked compartment. Finally, she removed a video-8 cassette from a box and passed a pen-sized scanner over the bar code on the cassette case, handed it to Jim without a word, then moved on to tend to other passengers. Jim popped the cassette into a player built into the armrest, and raised the personal screen that had become so popular with first-class travelers. He angled the screen away from the cabin, and slid the headphones over his ears. Jim Phelps settled back and sighed, but did not immediately push the start button. There were a few moments of hesitation as he stared out the window and thought about something that he did not reveal on his face.

When he finally did push the button to start the cassette, a sense of sadness, perhaps even boredom, flickered in his eyes.

A familiar face appeared on the screen.

This was Eugene Kittridge, Jim's boss, or "control," at CIA. Kittridge, like all career CIA men and women, had the kind of face that would blend in almost anywhere. Clean, neat, unemotional. Looking at him, it would be hard to guess that this was the face of a man who could order a building filled with civilians blown up in order to kill only one of them. In fact, Kittridge had the most dangerous kind of face of all, because it was impossible to read.

It was a recent development that the IMF team actually came under Kittridge's direct jurisdiction. When Jim Phelps, a former government operative himself, decided to run his own show by starting the IMF, his contacts at the CIA were more than happy to have a competent team of covert agents who could be called upon to perform missions that were too dangerous, or too perilous politically, to be officially sanctioned by any government agency. Jim Phelps assembled his own team, made his own rules, and called the shots every step of the way. But in the wake of the Aldrich Ames scandal, Eugene Kittridge was brought in to clean up the CIA's covert operations. He still wanted Jim Phelps and the IMF, but he wanted operational oversight of all the IMF missions. In return, he offered the deep pockets of the CIA black ops budget, a nonaccountable hundred-million-dollar-a-year fund used for the most sensitive CIA operations. Working for Kittridge allowed Phelps and the IMF to have access to the most recent, and costly, developments in technologies and intelligence. Times had changed and Phelps knew that the IMF had to change, too. Still, he didn't like the idea of having a boss, even though Jim retained the right to turn down any IMF assignment he felt uncomfortable with.

"Good morning, Mr. Phelps," Kittridge said. "The man you are about to see is Alexander Golitsyn." The image changed to a dark-haired man about forty, captured by a hidden camera. "Golitsyn is a former KGB line X officer now working the international black market selling intelligence. This morning we learned that Golitsyn has stolen one half of a CIA NOC list, the list of our nonofficial cover agents working in Eastern Europe."

A typewritten sample list, names and code names, scrolled rapidly across the screen.

"For security reasons," Kittridge continued, "the NOC list is divided into two encoded halves. Golitsyn already has the cryptonym portion, which contains agent code names and targeting areas. This portion is useless, however, unless combined with the second half—the true name list that is secured in the CIA station in our Prague embassy."

A stately building on the edge of the Vltava River, quite familiar to Jim, appeared on the screen.

"We have intelligence indicating that Golitsyn plans to steal the list at an embassy function tomorrow night. Your mission, should you decide to accept it, is to obtain photographic proof of the theft, apprehend Golitsyn and any co-conspirators, and return the stolen list. I'm sure I don't have to stress the importance of this matter, Jim. Because of its urgency, I've already dispatched to Prague a team selected from your usual group."

Other photographs popped on-screen: Jack Kiefer; Sarah Norman, a British woman; Hannah, a German with a very serious face; Claire Phelps; and Ethan.

"Ethan Hunt will be your point man, as usual."

Jim Phelps looked at the image of Ethan Hunt, then leaned back in the seat, closed his eyes in thought, and let out a deep breath. He'd been down many dangerous roads with Ethan Hunt, and had trusted him with his life more than once. Not only that, he entrusted Claire's well-being to Ethan and to no one else in the IMF. If Phelps had a protégé, then it would be Ethan. Yet, as close as he was to Ethan, Phelps couldn't say he knew him completely. Like all good agents, Ethan lived much of his life within himself, revealing only what was necessary when it was necessary. Just like Phelps.

When Jim opened his eyes Kittridge was back on-screen.

"As always, should you or any member of your IM Force be caught or killed, the secretary will disavow all knowledge of your actions. This tape will self-destruct in five seconds. Good luck, Jim."

Jim lit the Marlboro as the screen went blank. A wisp of smoke rose from the cassette player in the armrest as the tape began to incinerate itself, followed in a few seconds by a thin gray puff that signaled completion. As the smoke rose, Jim inhaled deeply off his cigarette, then blew a stream of smoke that blended with the cassette residue, forming a seamless cloud that floated to the cabin's ceiling.

And instead of stubbing out the cigarette, as he knew his wife would want him to, Jim relished the smoke. That smoking was still allowed on international flights was one of Jim's few pleasures during this otherwise joyless ride.

Prague

NINE WEEKS, NONSTOP, JIM," ETHAN SAID TO JIM PHELPS, as they stood in the kitchen of the IMF's safe house apartment in Prague. "I've been pushing this team right to the edge of the burner, and this mission we're talking about isn't a simple walk-through."

Phelps was tired from the long flight, his voice gravelly.

"I think you're being overly concerned."

"You pay me to be overly concerned," Ethan shot back, lowering his voice so that the other members of the team, working in the living room and dining room, wouldn't hear.

But the team members did hear, as well as see, what was going on in the kitchen, because their technical ops expert, Jack Kiefer, had left a pair of Visco glasses on the kitchen counter. The frames were slightly oversized, but not absurdly so, considering the complex microelectronics embedded within. They transmitted audio and video information through a nearly microscopic microphone and lens, and the signal could be monitored up to a mile away from the glasses, without utilizing complicated, sometimes detectable signal repeaters. Back in the living room, Jack Kiefer watched the confrontation on one of his small monitors. He wasn't too concerned; Ethan was always tense before a mission, and the arguments between Jim and Ethan had the tone of a father being challenged by his son, rather than a boss by his employee.

"If you don't think my plan is workable," Jim said to Ethan, "then let's hear why."

"It's an excellent plan."

"Thank you. Then?"

"Twenty-four hours ago Claire was under a heavy dose of that drug, and it's supposed to have a seventy-two-hour window of recovery. How do we know what the residual effect will be?"

"Claire's fine."

"Are you sure? You just got off an airplane, Jim."

Ethan turned away from him and began sliding passports and cash in various currencies into the false bottoms of cosmetics containers.

"Do you think I'd make a move if she wasn't fit and ready to work?"

"I'm not saying that."

"It sure sounds like that's what you're saying."

"I'm saying we're all tired."

"Everybody is off for three weeks after tonight. I can't reschedule this mission. You know it and I know it. I need my best team and you're it. So that's the schedule."

Jim was not taken aback by Ethan's anxiety. In fact, he welcomed it. He'd learned from over thirty years of this kind of work that the best agents asked questions. Of course, it did not escape him that the only operative Ethan seemed particularly worried about was Claire. Probably just jet lag, Jim thought, that made him think about these things. Or maybe the fact that he was twenty-five years Claire's senior, and Ethan was a handsome, dynamic kid that women liked at first sight. Maybe it was a sign of getting older that he concerned himself with any of these thoughts. But this wasn't the time for contemplation, he reminded himself.

"Ethan," he said, "was there a problem with the team in Kiev that you haven't debriefed?"

"No problems," Ethan said, almost too quickly; he was not about to go into the subject of Claire any further. He planned to complete the mission, take his vacation, and then maybe have a conversation with Jim, and suggest that it might be better all around if Claire was not assigned to his team anymore.

"It's your call," Jim said to Ethan after a long silence. "You tell me this team isn't ready, and I'll back off."

Ethan looked at Jim. They'd traveled too many roads together, were responsible for too many lives, to have this moment be about anything else but the truth.

"We're ready," Ethan said.

"Then I guess it's time to go to work?"

"Yeah."

Jim patted him on the shoulder, grabbed the Visco

27

glasses off the counter, and headed for the dining room, where the briefing area was set up.

"Show's over," Jim said lightly to Jack, tossing him the Visco glasses.

Jack shrugged, like he hadn't seen a thing.

The CIA maintained an ever-changing network of safe houses all over the world. They were available to Phelps and the IMF, but Phelps never used them. He always wanted to choose his own. Particularly for a mission as sensitive as this one.

The IMF team's Prague safe house was a small apartment, selected for its proximity to the embassy and its panoramic views. The place looked like it hadn't been remodeled since sometime between the two World Wars, but it suited the IMF's purposes.

Jack Kiefer had already swept the entire building with radio frequency monitors and additional equipment designed to detect electronic eavesdropping and video surveillance. He had installed additional state-of-the-art surveillance detection monitors, and had piggybacked power lines to ensure secure communication transmissions. He'd uplinked into CIA's communications satellites and had prepared backup security systems for all of the equipment. Kiefer's expertise and efficiency were such that the CIA refused to believe the IMF used only one tech ops guy on missions like this, and thought Phelps stonewalled them on the subject for internal security purposes. The truth was, when it came to electronics, it was always just Jack and his random genius.

For this particular mission, Kiefer installed enough technical equipment to make the safe house apartment look like NASA's mission control, and the team members were careful about where they put their feet amid the web of wiring. There were bags of food and other supplies scattered around the apartment, as well as dozens of foreign language newspapers, and a shredder in the center of the living room, into which somebody always seemed to be stuffing documents and instructions that had been committed to memory.

This certainly wasn't the tidiest apartment in Prague, but it was definitely the most interesting.

Seated next to Jack Kiefer was Sarah Norman, a Brit in her mid-thirties who spoke twenty-two languages convincingly. Hannah Wirth was a German who had earned Jim Phelps's respect by trailing a Hamas terrorist for six weeks, through nine countries and three time zones, never once losing track of him or ever being detected. At this moment Hannah was studying dossiers on every guest invited to the embassy party.

Claire Phelps sat in front of a computer, electronically traveling every street.

"Sarah, black us out," Jim Phelps said, pointing to the windows.

Sarah pulled the shades and plunged the room into darkness. Phelps hit a switch and two light boards flashed on, illuminating detailed schematics of the embassy. If there was any jet lag or doubt bothering Jim Phelps, it went away when he stood in front of his team. This was business, life and death, and in these matters he was always clear, concise, and confident.

"Very straightforward objective. We photograph Golitsyn accessing and copying the NOC list, track him to his buyer, and take both of them into custody.

If the buyer has backup, we're clear to neutralize opposition regardless of residual presence. Now here's the run—Ethan, you're going into the embassy in character, directly into the party with the highest possible profile. We're hiding you in plain sight. You okay with that?"

Ethan nodded at the end of the table. "Wouldn't have it any other way."

"Sarah," Phelps continued, "you're at the party as an embassy liaison from Washington. You'll make contact with Ethan and run the show together."

"Couldn't possibly, Jim," Sarah answered lightly, "haven't a thing to wear."

"You'll work it out. Once you're inside, mark Golitsyn, then Hannah, you'll be following Golitsyn through the party."

He turned to Jack, who seemed to be nodding off.

"Jack, you with us?"

Jack's head snapped up, and Phelps stared him down. "The NOC list is in the basement, a secured area only accessible to a few official cover agency people. There's the classic 'denied' area," he continued, pointing to the schematic, "and access to that room is controlled by a thumbprint scanner outside the elevator. Jack, you'll be inside the shaft making certain that Sarah passes the thumbprint scanner, and then you'll control elevator movement."

"Guess I won't be wearing a tux to the party," Jack said.

"I guess not," Jim said. "Open. Close. Get out. Zero residual presence."

"What's new," Jack said.

"Nothing," Phelps replied, turning to his wife.

"Claire, you're exterior transport. Hannah will join you once Golitsyn heads for the denied area. If Golitsyn has a car waiting, you stay with him. If he rolls, forget us and stay with him no matter what. And I recommend you spend the afternoon cruising the streets in the Little Quarter. They're confusing as hell." His tone softened as he spoke to his wife, and those who knew Phelps well, like Ethan and Jack, saw the flicker of concern in his eyes.

Claire smiled at her husband. "What do you think I did all morning?"

Jim faced the team. "We're spread out on this one, so if anything goes wrong, I call for an abort and we walk away. Immediately. Regroup here at four A.M. That's oh–four hundred. Any questions?"

"Yeah," Ethan said, cutting the ensuing silence. "Can we get a cappuccino machine in here? 'Cause I don't know what you call *this* . . ." He held up the Styrofoam cup of coffee that he'd been drinking.

Jack agreed. "I call it cruel and unusual."

"Hey, I made that," Claire said.

"Is it possible it's even worse than the sludge we had to drink in that barn in Kiev?" Ethan asked the group.

Phelps cracked the smallest of smiles, pleased to see that Ethan was settling into the mission.

"So, Jim," Ethan continued in a deadpan voice, "we sure as hell missed you in Kiev. You off on one of those cushy recruiting assignments again? Where'd they put you up for this one? The Plaza?"

"Drake Hotel," Jim said, pleased with himself. "Chicago."

"Oh, how punishing," Jack said. "Twenty-four-

31

hour room service. Towels as thick as a porterhouse steak."

"Chauffeured cars," Ethan said.

"Expense account," Jack threw in.

"He's getting soft in his old age," Ethan added.

"Okay, listen up," Jim said, acknowledging the digs with a friendly nod. "If that list gets out in the open, the names of our agents in every country in Eastern Europe will be up for grabs to the highest bidders. That means the list goes to terrorists, arms dealers, drug lords—anybody and everybody who'd like to get rid of long-term coverts just like us. If they're exposed, they'll be executed. Nowhere to hide."

The team grew very still. Each of them knew at least half a dozen people on that NOC list.

"I'll call the shots from the command post here. I have video feed from each sector. Now let's get specific. Ethan?" Phelps pointed to Claire's computer as she brought up a quick-time video clip of *The McLaughlin Report* from American television. John McLaughlin was interviewing a southern senator, immediately recognizable to everyone in the room: Senator Richard Waltzer.

"I'll go you one further," the senator was saying to McLaughlin. "I say the CIA and all its shadow organizations have become irrelevant at best and unconstitutional at worst. The Cold War is over. Let's stop playing spy games and put all that money to more productive uses. It's time we throw a little light on the whole concept of the Pentagon's so-called 'black budget.' These covert agency subgroups have confidential funding, they report to no one. *Who are these people?*"

The digitized playback ended. Ethan looked at Jim. "You're going to use Waltzer?"

"He's our guy."

"Isn't he chairing Armed Services hearings this week?"

"Next week. This week he's fly-fishing at the Oughterard Slough in County Kildare, with one of my best Irish guides."

"I see."

"Think you have enough time to make it work?"

"He's going to be a pleasure." Ethan smiled. Even though this mission was all business, Senator Waltzer was just the kind of politician Ethan liked to mess with. He knew that Waltzer's anti-CIA rhetoric was fodder for the voters back home, and when it came time for a Senate vote on funding, Waltzer was right there toeing the party line. Waltzer represented the Washington double-talk that had disillusioned Ethan years ago when he served in Special Forces and then CIA black ops teams. Ethan served his country with patriotic intention, but once he entered covert global fieldwork, he quickly learned that politicians often sanctioned secret missions for motives that were far from patriotic, that had more to do with protecting the interests of certain corporations or facilitating hidden political agendas. When all of this duplicity became clear to Ethan he left government service and was approached by Jim Phelps for the IMF team. At IMF, Phelps assured Ethan, he would always know the purpose of the mission and would never suffer repercussions if he chose not to participate in a particular mission. Phelps helped transition Ethan out of the CIA to embark on a training process that raised Ethan's game to new levels of sophistication.

Ethan was Phelps's prize pupil, to the point where he became the IMF's point man on the most critical missions, and was entrusted with deep background briefings from Jim that no one else at IMF was privy to. And Ethan Hunt was the quickest study that Phelps had ever met. Besides being multilingual, Ethan had a talent for imitating voices and copying mannerisms. From studying the short videotape, he would master enough of Senator Waltzer's traits to pass himself off to unsuspecting local dignitaries. Jack Kiefer and Sarah Norman were already at work on the latex and Mylopar mask for Ethan, and by the time Ethan walked out of the safe house, he could probably fool half of Waltzer's constituents.

Jack signaled Ethan to come over to his work station, then opened a box that Jim had brought in from the States. It was the IMF's newest tool: bubble gum. "If you come up against a lock tonight that you can't pick," he said to Ethan, "here's the last way out." He unwrapped from a foil packet what looked like a conventional stick of gum, except that one half of it was red, the other green. "Red light, green light," Jack said slowly. "Mash them together—hasta lasagna, don't get any on ya. You have five seconds."

Ethan took the pack of gum.

Jack smiled. "Just don't chew it, or all those years in braces will have been a damn waste."

The Mission

CLAIRE PHELPS LOOKED IN THE REARVIEW MIRROR OF THE BMW sedan she was driving to see the sixty-year-old southern gentleman with grayish white hair, a sun-blotched complexion, and gold-frame glasses who sat in the backseat. He wore a white tuxedo and spoke softly to himself with a southern accent. The transformation of Ethan Hunt into Senator Richard Waltzer amazed even her.

As the sedan pulled through the gates of the U.S. Embassy, Ethan continued to quietly practice the accent, reciting the names of several people on the guest list to whom he might be introduced. At the same time, he peered out the window at the fog that was building over the Vltava River.

Two variables Ethan Hunt didn't like when on a mission: cars that malfunctioned and changes in weather. Even though the IMF team always had backup cars in case of mechanical difficulties, their missions often hinged on split-second timing, and a reluctant engine created problems. The weather was more difficult to plan around. High winds and rain interfered with disguises and microelectronic devices, which is why the team preferred working at night, when the effects of sudden changes in weather might at least be mitigated by darkness.

But as the car rolled to a stop in front of the embassy, Ethan took a second look at the night sky. The fog had begun as a low-lying mist that hovered above the Vltava River, but now it seemed to be gradually thickening and rising. And the potential problem that crossed Ethan's mind had to do with the labyrinthine network of tiny streets around the embassy, and the possibility of Golitsyn getting out in the open. This was a fact that he filed away with a thousand other facts pertaining to the mission, as Claire flashed fake credentials to the marine guard who approached the car.

Ethan stepped out of the sedan and returned the guard's crisp salute, looking past him in order to pick a route up the stairs and into the building that would avoid the most people.

Jack Kiefer was already inside, dressed in black, slipping into the elevator shaft that would provide access to the denied-area room in the basement where the NOC list was stored on computer. Jack looked insectlike, wearing the largest model of black-rimmed Visco glasses, which covered half his face.

"I'm in," he whispered into his mouthpiece. "How's the picture?"

"Outstanding. Good job," Jim Phelps answered from his command post at the safe house.

Phelps sat in front of two computers that windowed the Visco views of each of his field operatives. The name of each team member was boxed just below the transmission view from their Visco glasses. Phelps could already see various views of the embassy party transmitted by Hannah and Sarah, and he followed Ethan's point of view as he exited the car and walked into the lobby.

Firing up a Marlboro, Jim sucked in a huge draw of smoke and leaned forward, watching all five transmissions. When the mission was complete he would open all the windows in the safe house and air the place out, so that Claire wouldn't lecture him about smoking; but the cigarette at the launch of a mission was a ritualistic good-luck charm for Phelps, and after all these years he wasn't about to shuffle a winning hand.

"Ethan," Jim said into his microphone, "Jack's inside. Window's open by twenty-three hundred."

Ethan's only reply was to look casually at his watch, and that picture alone was Jim's acknowledgment.

Jack climbed a narrow metal ladder in the shaft and found the metal boxes that housed the elevator controls and the brains to the security system that allowed access to the elevator. He flicked on his face-mounted halogen tube light and went to work. Contained in the pockets of his jumpsuit was enough electronic equipment to start a medium-sized repair shop. But he knew the precise position of each tool and its purpose; there wasn't a single wasted motion as he worked.

A creaking sound from above caught his attention. He looked up. The elevator car was stationed three stories above him, and the old metal box was emitting some sort of noise. "That thing looks older than the building, if that's possible," Jack whispered. "And I don't think this ladder has been inspected since World War Two."

"Keep going," Phelps said. "You're right on schedule."

Jack patched several wires into the control box and installed an infrared transmitter that interfaced with his portable computer. In a few minutes, Sarah Norman would escort Senator Waltzer on a tour of the facility, and she would be required to place her thumbprint in a scanner to allow access to the elevator and basement denied area. Since she wasn't in the embassy's approved security databank, Jack needed to override the security system on her behalf; he had to be ready when Sarah's thumb went into the scanner or the mission would collapse. The seconds ticked away.

As he worked he heard the orchestra that played in the embassy ballroom, transmitted through Sarah's, Hannah's, and Ethan's glasses. "Hey, that's beautiful music," Jack said. "Makes me proud to be a taxpayer."

"How long?" Phelps asked, watching his computer screens.

"These elevator electronics aren't of this century," Jack said. "I guess the State Department ran out of money when they refurbished this place."

Phelps fired up another Marlboro and watched Jack

work, listening to Jack hum along with the band. "Remember this one?" Jack asked. "It was a hit when kaiser helmets were still popular."

Jack studied the code numbers on chips inside the control box and finally found a microprocessor labeled P-12 that was the size of a postage stamp. His humming suddenly started sounding happier.

Until he heard a loud *clank.*

Inside the embassy Ethan also heard it in his earpiece. Phelps heard it back at the safe house.

Jack looked over his shoulder, then down, thinking the metal ladder was cracking. But then another loud clank. Coming from above.

The elevator was moving. Directly toward Jack.

He looked down, decided against a leap or a mad scramble down the ladder. He grabbed the ladder and swung his body into the vertical gutter that ran the length of the shaft, jamming himself in as tight as possible.

The elevator car slid down next to him, brushing his shoulder blades.

Then it stopped.

Jack was pinned, his face jammed halfway into the control panel, his left eyeball practically touching the P-12 chip that needed to be replaced if he hoped to override the security system. If that chip stayed where it was, Sarah could leave her thumb on the scanner until the next millennium and not get access approval, and Senator Waltzer wouldn't get any closer to the denied area than the violin player in the embassy orchestra.

"Jim?" Jack said calmly. "You seeing this?"

* * *

As he entered the ballroom, Ethan knew from Jack's tone that there was a problem, but since he was portraying the amiable visiting senator, he could show nothing on his face.

"Senator, I'm Rand Housman, the ambassador's aide," said an overanxious Ivy Leaguer who grabbed Ethan's right hand. "It's very much an honor to have you all the way over here, and it would be my pleasure to take you through the receiving line. We have quite a group waiting to meet you."

Before Ethan could slip away, the aide had him by the elbow and steered him to a reception line.

Sarah Norman quickly crossed the room and closed in on Ethan.

"Senator, allow me to introduce the director of the National Gallery, Mr. Jaroslav Reid," Housman said. "And here is Mr. Peter Brandl, the mayor of Prague."

Sarah didn't want to risk any more introductions. She stepped forward and reached for the senator's hand, breaking into a charming, shy smile. "I'll bet you don't remember me, do you, Senator?"

Ethan looked at her for a convincingly long moment.

"I'm going to surprise you and tell you I do," he replied. "Miss Norman, isn't it?"

He leaned forward and gave her a polite hug.

"Golitsyn's in pocket," she whispered into his ear, "under the archway behind me."

Ethan nodded.

Then they both heard Jim Phelps in their earpieces.

"Mark the target," Phelps said to Sarah. "Phase two."

"Your office made me promise a tour," Sarah said to Senator Waltzer, "and I've got that set up for you."

"Well, very good," Ethan replied, in Waltzer's southern drawl, "let's get going."

He turned to Rand Housman. "Will you excuse us a few moments, and then I'm all yours."

The young embassy aide nodded, confused but unwilling to question a United States senator, particularly one with a reputation for having a whipcrack temper.

Sarah skillfully worked Ethan across the room, keeping just out of reach of those who might want to introduce themselves.

They had Golitsyn in sight, a tall, dark-haired man who was wearing a beautifully cut tuxedo, looking very much the diplomat rather than covert operative. But since Golitsyn paid that kind of precise attention to detail, Sarah knew she would have to be cautious as she approached him. Without having to share a word with Sarah, Ethan knew exactly what she was thinking, and they timed their approach to Golitsyn to occur when a waiter was nearby, passing canapés. Ethan made a show of looking over the food so that Golitsyn would take a second look as well. And as he did, Sarah deftly misted the back of Golitsyn's head with a brief burst from a perfume bottle, making it appear that she was applying the fragrance to herself. The entire transaction took only two seconds and went off flawlessly, but it was a move that Ethan and Sarah had rehearsed and executed a thousand times.

"Package is marked, Hannah," Jim Phelps said from his command post. "Pull the shade."

Hannah was positioned halfway up the sweeping marble stairway, a vantage point from which she surveyed the entire reception room. At Jim's order, she touched a tiny hinge on the frame of her glasses, causing the lenses to perceptibly change hue, and with them her perspective of the room became deeply shaded. Suddenly she saw the world as if through night-vision glasses. The back of Golitsyn's head glowed a fluorescent lime green where it had been marked by Sarah's spray.

"Package is lit," Hannah said.

"Stay with him," Jim replied.

At the top of the second-floor stairway Sarah and Ethan veered left, crossing a short hallway where the elevator was blocked by a sign indicating that it was out of service for the evening.

Sarah headed directly for it.

Before she could ask Jack if the scanner was successfully overridden, Sarah was intercepted by a marine guard in dress blues who appeared from behind the security station door.

"Excuse me," he said, "but this area of the embassy is out of service for the duration of the evening."

Sarah quickly shifted into her role as Senator Waltzer's guide. ". . . which, Senator, leads directly to the denied area in the basement, the only limited-access area in the entire facility."

"Well, let's see what our funding is providing, shall we?" Ethan said.

She pulled an ID card from her purse and flashed it at the guard. "And I think you know Senator Waltzer," she continued smoothly.

The guard saluted but did not leave.

"As you can see," Sarah went on to Ethan, "this area has a guard station and video surveillance, and is monitored twenty-four hours a day."

"I hope we pay you soldiers overtime," Ethan said.

"It's an honor to serve my country, sir," the marine said.

"Yes, it is," Ethan answered.

Jim Phelps monitored the situation on his screens, but couldn't risk speaking, with the marine standing right there in the otherwise quiet hallway.

Sarah placed her thumb on the scanner slot adjacent to the elevator doors. A small screen above the scanner flashed its decision: ACCESS DENIED.

She fluffed off the error message and tried again, looking apologetically at the senator for the momentary inconvenience.

The implacable guard stood rock steady.

"Senator," Sarah said, replacing her thumb on the scanner, "don't you have a young man on your staff named Jack?"

"Jack. I believe we did have a young man named Jack. For a time, anyway. Not a reliable man, as I recall. Constantly late or behind in his work. I won't tolerate that on my staff."

"Nor should you," Sarah said.

"I'm sorry, ma'am," the guard said, stepping closer, "but I'll have to recheck your identification. Pardon me, Senator."

Sarah looked at Ethan.

"Keep dancing," Jim Phelps whispered.

"Never apologize for doing your job, soldier," Ethan said to the marine. "Now this young man, Jack, since he didn't do his job, we were forced to tie him to

43

my best stallion and drag him around the barn a few times. Did no good at all."

Sarah pressed her thumb to the scanner a second time. Again: ACCESS DENIED.

What the hell do you think I'm doing in here, taking a coffee break?, Jack wanted to scream. He remained wedged between the elevator and the metal gutter, arms pinned against his sides. Jack Kiefer had spent the better part of his adult life in narrow crawl spaces, heating ducts, car trunks, sewer pipes, utility tunnels, and other claustrophobic infrastructures in every civilized country in the world. He was used to it, even trained for it. But in this case he was less prepared than usual, because that elevator wasn't supposed to move until he told it to. The first thing Jack had done in the shaft was override the system controls so that only he or Jim Phelps could operate it. But obviously it had malfunctioned. This was Prague. The electronics were only as good as the support systems built into the building, and God only knew what ancient labyrinth of circuitry this building hid.

When he heard the electronic clicks coming from the scanner being accessed by Sarah's thumb, Jack knew he had only seconds before the mission would have to be aborted. And it was a matter of professional pride with him that an abort not be triggered by his link in the chain.

Kiefer sucked in a huge breath of air and then exhaled what felt like every molecule of oxygen in his body, in an effort to make himself as thin as possible. He slid down the gutter, feeling the cab of the elevator scraping the back of his head. The ancient metal ladder rung gave way beneath his feet, and to keep from plunging down the shaft he thrust his knees forward and jammed himself between the cab and the wall.

He reached up to the control box. Jack couldn't see inside the box now, he could work only by feel. Fortunately, as part of his preparation, he had committed the schematic of the box to memory, and like an expert soldier who can disassemble and reassemble his rifle in the dark, Jack was able to work blind. Running his fingers over the various chips in the control box, he stopped on P-12. At least, it'd better be P-12, because if he pulled the wrong chip the system would lock down and require special codes—codes that neither he nor Phelps had—to reboot. It was time for commitment. Jack pulled the chip and let it drop into his sleeve.

He heard the guard asking to recheck Sarah's ID. She'd struck out twice on the scanner. She'd be lucky to get a third try. He deftly picked a replacement chip from his pocket, clipped two tiny electrodes to it, then ran his fingers back to the box.

Watching the monitors, Jim Phelps sucked a Marlboro down to its ash.

Pushing the replacement chip into its socket, Jack reached to the top of the elevator cab and did a gritty pull-up that made three of his ribs feel like they had cracked. Gasping for air from the pain in his chest, he slid the subnotebook from its slot, flipped it open. It lit up with a picture of Sarah's ID on one half of the screen, and her thumbprint on the other.

Jack heard Ethan talking about somebody named Jack being dragged by horses around a barn, and at this particular moment he thought he might prefer that scenario to this one.

"Downloading," Jack whispered, cringing from the pain in his ribs.

In the hallway, Sarah maintained her breezy, inconvenienced demeanor and dropped her thumb on the scanner, just as the marine was again staring at her ID. A faint bell sounded, and the security readout screen glowed green with the legend: IDENTITY CONFIRMED.

The marine looked at the screen and seemed relieved not to have to deny a United States senator access to an American embassy post.

The elevator doors slipped open, and Sarah and Ethan stepped on board.

The marine snapped another salute, which Ethan acknowledged.

Above them, Jack Kiefer had crawled to the air grate on the top of the elevator cab. He looked down at his two colleagues.

Everyone was too relieved to say a word.

Phelps came on-line, business as usual. He checked his monitors and didn't have sight of Golitsyn. "Hannah, I'm blind again," he said. "Where's the package?"

"Headed to the denied area."

The elevator opened into the basement security room. It was a very basic setup, nothing like the sophisticated rooms the techs from Langley set up at other embassies. In fact, as Ethan scanned the room he was surprised that this modest arrangement of computers, filing cabinets, and storage vaults would be entrusted with the NOC list, encrypted or not. But, like every other government outfit, the CIA could be penny-wise and pound-foolish. Golitsyn evidently had identified a soft spot, and chose to access the Prague embassy for the very reasons Ethan surmised—minimal resistance.

Ethan handed his Visco glasses to Sarah and dashed to the main computer terminal. He strapped on a watch-size Visco monitor and motioned to Sarah to set the glasses in position.

Golitsyn was on the move, which meant Ethan and Sarah had to be in and out of there quickly.

She placed the glasses upside-down on a filing cabinet and awaited Ethan's response. He sat in front of the terminal, exactly where Golitsyn would have to sit in order to access the computer, and checked the picture being broadcast from the glasses to his wrist monitor.

"Higher," he said to Sarah, checking the picture on his wrist monitor.

She followed his direction.

"That's it. Right there. Jim?"

"Receiving," Jim acknowledged, then added, "but get moving, Golitsyn is rolling to you."

Ethan and Sarah rushed to the elevator door, waiting for Jack to open it.

But the elevator started moving upward.

"Jack, we're in position, let's go," Ethan said urgently.

But in the shaft Jack sat atop the elevator, staring at his computer screen in disbelief. He executed three keystrokes, but the elevator kept moving up.

"There's a short," Jack said, "I didn't signal a move."

The elevator door opened and Alexander Golitsyn stepped inside and hit the basement button. Jack saw him through the grate, which meant Jim Phelps was seeing Golitsyn on his monitor.

"He's in the box, Ethan," Phelps said, concerned. "The package is in the box."

There was no exit from the basement room other than the elevator, or down the shaft.

"We've got to go under," Ethan said.

"I'm opening the safety doors," Jim Phelps replied, trying his override buttons. The elevator's safety doors opened, revealing the empty shaft. But the elevator itself was now moving downward, carrying Golitsyn.

"Stop the box," Ethan said to both Jack and Jim.

"If we stop it, Golitsyn will spook," Phelps said. "Go."

Ethan and Sarah looked at the black hole beneath them.

No time to do anything else. Ethan grabbed Sarah's hand and they leaped into the darkness, landing hard on the cement floor eight feet below. Sarah scrambled to her feet but Ethan pulled her back down as the elevator came to a stop just inches above their heads.

Ethan lifted his wrist monitor and watched Golitsyn cross quickly to the computer terminal, slip on cloth-lined latex gloves, and go to work. Thirty seconds later Golitsyn dropped a diskette into the A drive and began downloading the NOC file. A minute later he had his copy and shoved the diskette into a plastic box.

Ethan signaled Sarah to move toward the small service door at the base of the shaft. They crawled to it and pushed it open and exited into an area of trash receptacles. He ripped his mask off while Sarah reconned the area. Ethan wiped his face with a special solvent-moistened towelette, dumped the mask in a trash bin, and sprayed it with another solvent that melted the mask into an unrecognizable goo. So much for the esteemed Senator Waltzer.

Already on the move out of the area, he pulled off his tuxedo jacket and turned it inside out to reveal a different color. Suddenly he looked like Ethan Hunt again, grabbing Sarah's hand and walking with her toward the river walk next to the embassy.

Smiling at Sarah like she was the love of his life, Ethan lifted his wrist monitor and spoke to Jack Kiefer.

"Have you got control of the elevator doors?"

"Should have," came Jack's answer.

"Good. Claire, transport ready?"

"Roger," came Claire's response from inside the waiting car.

"Base, how's the picture of our package?" Ethan asked Phelps.

"Perfect recording," Jim answered.

Ethan next checked Hannah. "Stairway, you're clear, go to transport."

"Moving," Hannah said, flicking her glasses back to normal, heading for the embassy's rear exit.

"Okay, we're in position," Ethan said. "Jack, open the doors and let the package roll."

"Roger that," Jack said. "Opening doors now."

Despite the delays with the elevator and security scanner electronics, the mission was working. Golitsyn's theft was captured on digitized video, and

Jim Phelps was already sending the pictures via satellite to Langley. Now it was time to apprehend Golitsyn and recover the diskette.

"Doors not responding," Jack said, retracing his wiring from the laptop to the control panel.

Golitsyn pushed the call button several times, and became concerned when the elevator didn't respond. Had he been detected? Was he trapped in the denied area?

Then the elevator started moving.

But not down to the basement like it was supposed to.

The elevator started moving up with a short, sudden lurch.

"Hey," Jack said quietly.

Ethan Hunt knew Jack's voice, and this "hey" was not Jack being funny. Something clearly had gone wrong.

Jim Phelps knew it instantly, looking at his monitor.

"Jack? What are you doing?" Phelps asked.

"Nothing. That's my problem. It's moving on its own."

Jim punched a few keys from his end. Nothing happened.

Down in the basement Golitsyn heard the elevator moving and saw that it was not descending. Like Ethan, Golitsyn knew that there was a service door in the bottom of the shaft. It was time to execute his own contingency plan. He pried the elevator's safety doors open and leaped into the shaft. He pulled a tiny flashlight from his pocket and noted that the security lights on the service doors were inactive. With no time to question it, he opened them.

The elevator, with Jack still perched on its roof, continued to move upward.

Jack furiously worked his keyboard.

"No good," he said to Jim. "Go to override. Repeat, go to override."

"I'm trying," Jim responded. "I don't have it. I don't have control!"

"Then I have a real problem," he said to Jim, looking up to see the dim ceiling of the elevator shaft, barely two floors overhead, and closing in.

Ethan's voice cut through the microspeaker of Jack's Visco glasses. "Cut the power," he said, his voice low and tense. "Cut the power, Jack. Do you hear me? Just shut it all down."

Jack nodded, reaching for the backup control box atop the elevator that activated the emergency power switch. He ripped the lid off the box.

"Come on, Jack," Ethan hissed, looking at the wrist monitor. "Now."

Jack ripped away wires in the box, eviscerating the entire system.

But the elevator kept moving. He looked up.

The elevator passed a trip switch and a grid of yard-long, pointed spikes snapped down from the ceiling at the top of the shaft. Both Ethan and Phelps saw the sudden glint of sharp steel in the shaft.

"Now, Jack, now!" Ethan yelled.

Jack ripped every wire, tube, box, and connection out of that control panel, all to no effect. He looked up again and the last thing he saw—and the last thing

Ethan and Phelps saw—was the first row of spikes slamming into his back. The scream of agony echoed in the microspeakers as Jack's transmission went to static.

"Jack," Ethan whispered. "Jack!" he repeated, not ready to accept what his eyes and ears had just recorded.

Ethan turned to Sarah with eyes so full of emotion that she froze.

"Man down," Jim Phelps said, confused and angry. "I'm on the way."

Ethan heard Jim bolt out of the safe house, the door slamming shut behind him.

Abort

ALEXANDER GOLITSYN, THE NOC LIST SAFELY STORED IN his inside breast pocket, paused in the trash area outside the elevator's service door. He brushed off his tux, straightened his hair, and lit a cigarette. Double-checking the embassy's exterior security cameras—he knew their positions and the precise angles at which they were pointed—Golitsyn began walking on a preplanned trajectory designed to dissuade anyone who happened to be checking the monitors from noticing that this tuxedoed stroller was actually emerging from the embassy's trash area. From Golitsyn's point of view, the two attractive people leaning against the wall twenty yards away were a romantic couple enjoying themselves and the lights sparkling on the river. A faint flash of light coming from the man's wristwatch seemed to be only a reflection from a nearby street lamp.

Instead, it was Ethan Hunt checking his Visco monitor, responding to Jim Phelps who panted, "I'm en route, initiating Viscos."

The image on Ethan's monitor was blurring and jumbled; Jim was running full tilt. Even so, Ethan recognized the Charles Bridge coming into Jim's view. Suddenly the view swung around wildly; Jim was looking over his shoulder as he ran, and the rear view was becoming shrouded in fog. Ethan glanced back at the river and saw the dense, white, billowy fog rising and spreading; visibility was rapidly deteriorating—exactly what Ethan feared might happen.

Sarah grabbed Ethan's arm and pointed to the riverbank walkway in front of the embassy. There, navigating quickly through a throng of people leaving the party, was Golitsyn.

Ethan flicked on the audio pickup of his monitor.

"Jim! Jim! The package is in the open."

"Where?"

"West riverbank, moving north."

Jim's next reply was unexpected. "I've got a shadow."

Ethan followed Golitsyn with his eyes. "Can you lose him?"

"No. Abort."

"Ethan," Sarah said, watching Golitsyn move away from the crowd and quicken his pace, "he's out of pocket."

Ethan barked into his wrist monitor, "Jim, we can't."

"Abort," Phelps said angrily. "That's an order."

"Negative! Golitsyn's on the move."

54

"No, dammit, no, this is an *abort!* Repeat, abort! Claire, ready transport."

Two blocks away Claire Phelps sat in the transport car, listening to Jim and Ethan argue. "Transport ready," she replied. She'd heard the two men argue in the past. But never in the field. Not during a mission. Jim had issued an order.

Ethan turned to Sarah. "Eye on the package." Into his monitor he said, "Jim, I'm coming to you."

Sarah held Ethan's arm firmly. "Jim gave the abort," she argued. "This is when we walk away."

But Ethan's eyes were focused and flaming. "No, we're going to recover the disk, understand?! Now move!"

Ethan sprinted toward the Charles Bridge.

Sarah hesitated, then took off after Golitsyn. She could still vaguely see his black form moving through the fog along the riverbank, and she picked up her pace to close the gap between them, passing a drunken young couple who had been engaged in a loud argument.

Ethan, fast approaching the bridge, heard a squawk from his monitor and pressed it to his ear.

"Where are you?" Jim demanded.

"Two hundred yards."

"They're covering this frequency, Ethan," Jim panted. "Cut all radio communication. Repeat, cut all radio communication."

Nearing the steps to the bridge, Ethan charged past Claire in the transport vehicle. Her hands were on the wheel and gearshift, ready to leave the moment the team arrived.

Ethan checked his monitor.

Jim was at the other side of the bridge, not running anymore, but peering over his shoulder through the rising fog. Suddenly the scene whirled around. Perfectly visible on the tiny screen was the barrel of a gun aimed point-blank at Jim. A tiny, static-filled pop burst from the microspeaker and the transmission went momentarily crazy. Then, with frightening steadiness, Jim's point of view shifted, his head tilted down.

There was a bloody hole in the center of Jim's chest.

"Jim!" Ethan shouted, sprinting again.

The scene on the monitor swooped up, then down. Jim was staggering toward the bridge's railing. The dark face of the river flashed into view.

Jim was falling.

Ethan tore through the fog, scanning the bridge for the shooter. But he saw no one else. He leaned over the railing and looked down at the dark, choppy water that was now barely visible.

No sign at all of Jim. Even if he was alive, the icy river water would kill him in minutes.

Ethan heard sounds along the promenade. He ran toward the end of the bridge and saw Golitsyn walking briskly. Ethan started to give chase, glancing back at the transport vehicle, where he saw Claire's outline in the driver's seat. And in the instant while Ethan thought about what he was going to say to her, there was a massive explosion.

The car blew twenty feet into the air and turned into a rolling fireball.

The force of the blast knocked Ethan backward as

the mushroom cloud of flames illuminated the riverbank like daylight.

"Claire!" Ethan screamed, covering up from raining glass and debris.

A crowd of onlookers quickly formed, gawking at the inferno of twisted metal.

Sarah heard the explosion and saw the flash of light through the fog. Still, she stayed with Golitsyn, moving at a jog to keep up with his rapid progress.

There was no doubt in Sarah's mind that the explosion involved the IMF team, and she worried that Ethan's ignoring Jim's order to abort might have had tragic consequences. But Ethan had run point on a hundred missions involving Sarah. She knew he did not take stupid risks; he made quick, calculated decisions. And this certainly wasn't the time to start second-guessing him. Alexander Golitsyn carried a disk that was key to hundreds of lives and a thousand covert operations; it was Sarah's task to keep him in sight until Ethan returned, and that's what she intended to do.

Ahead, Golitsyn finally slowed down, reaching some kind of marker or rendezvous point. He edged toward an archway and seemed to speak with another person hiding in the alley.

Sarah eased her pace and walked on the balls of her feet so as to make no sound on the cobblestone street. And at that moment she, too, realized that she was being followed. She glanced over her shoulder and through the fog recognized the drunken couple who had been arguing near the embassy. They were still fighting, but quietly now, and walking. Sarah did not believe in coincidences in matters involving espionage. She turned back in time to see Golitsyn suddenly straighten up, then crumple to the ground. As Golitsyn's body fell, Sarah saw an arm reach from behind the archway and pull something from Golitsyn's jacket. The disk. Sarah ran forward, pulling from her purse a thick pen that contained a single titanium-tipped projectile filled with a lethal chemical; it was capable of firing a single round, potent enough to stop a charging bear. But when she reached Golitsyn's body, there was no one in the archway or in the alley. She turned him over to see the red stain on his tuxedo shirt, just below the sternum, indicating a perfectly aimed, upward thrust from a fierce blade. Sarah heard footsteps running on the cobblestone street, but they seemed to be approaching rather than receding. Ethan, no doubt. But just as she turned her head, she caught a sudden, swift blur out of the corner of her right eye, and she felt herself punched in the chest, and the figure of a man who seemed to materialize out of the fog was gone just as quickly as he had appeared.

At first, she thought the wind was knocked out of her, because she couldn't catch her breath. Sarah doubled over, trying to suck in air. But as her chin tilted down she felt a hot, salty mist in her throat; she coughed out a breath and with it came blood. And she saw something protruding from her chest, the handle of a knife. The calm, detached sensation that enveloped her body, Sarah realized, was shock.

Ethan burst out of the fog as Sarah half fell, half sat

down on the wet cobblestones. He ran to her, knelt, and lifted her head.

She looked at him, expressionless. Then Ethan saw the knife. And in the instant her eyes met his, Sarah knew from his stunned expression that she was dying. He slid the knife out of her chest; it had a long, serrated blade. The last thing she saw was the drunken Russian couple who had stopped across the street in the foggy shadows, and at this point they didn't seem so drunk; they seemed very intent on watching her. And Sarah thought how stupid it was to die in this foreign city with two strangers staring at her from across the street. The fog seemed to crystallize and sparkle in Sarah's eyes as she felt consciousness lifting away.

Then she died.

Ethan gently lowered her head back down to the ground, stood, and examined the knife for any telltale markings. He set it on the ground and moved to Golitsyn. A quick inspection of his pockets turned up nothing. Not a key, a coin, or even a piece of lint.

Sirens pierced the quiet of the night. Distant, but closing. A Prague police boat, lights flashing, docked at the bank beside the embassy. Several officers leaped off the boat and sprinted toward the burning car. Another police boat approached from the opposite direction and these officers jumped ashore and ran down the promenade.

Ethan looked at Golitsyn, then at Sarah. Blood soaked their clothes.

There was nothing else for Ethan to do. No transport. No backup.

"Hannah," he called into his Visco monitor. "Hannah!"

No answer. He was breathing hard, perspiration flowing down his face. Ethan whirled around to see policemen charging through the fog.

It was time to run.

Kittridge

Ethan Hunt RAN THROUGH THE WET, DARK STREETS OF Prague, avoiding lights, busy streets, and curious eyes.

There were young people here from all over the world. Word was out that Prague was like Paris in the twenties, filled with expatriates and students trying to make some sense of a world they weren't quite ready to plug into. Accommodations and food were cheap, dozens of small newspapers flourished around town, coffeehouses and bars filled nightly with kids wanting to talk politics, music, and sex, and at night, the streets teemed with young people.

Ethan looked warily at the youths bopping in out of the bars, laughing and having a good time; as far as he was concerned, the disaster of the embassy mission still screaming inside his brain, any of these people could be dangerous. He felt a stony isolation from everyone and anyone who crossed his path. Ethan was shaken and seething as he replayed each moment of the mission in his photographic memory and searched the sickeningly vivid images for clues as to what might have happened.

Claire was dead.

Jim was dead.

Jack, Sarah, and, most likely, Hannah were dead as well.

And it was Ethan who had defied Jim's order to abort, yet he was still alive. There had been missions in the past that were aborted for one reason or another; sometimes a last-second call from Langley that came without comment or explanation stopped a mission in progress. Sometimes the abort signal came only because Jim or Ethan smelled a trap. That was the nature of IMF work. But Golitsyn was walking away with the NOC list, the CIA's most confidential file, a file that, Ethan knew, simply couldn't get out into the open without catastrophic consequences. So he had ignored Jim's order, and had made a judgment call from his position as point man in the field.

But it had all gone terribly wrong. And certainly it was far from over. There were procedures to be followed in the event of this kind of emergency, beginning with a phone call.

It took him a while, but he finally found a lone phone booth outside a building on an empty street on the outskirts of the student quarter. He unscrewed the phone's mouthpiece and from his pocket produced a flat metal disk with six silver prongs protruding from one of its sides. Ethan popped the prongs into the exposed mouthpiece and screwed the cover back on. The prongs melded into the wiring, and suddenly the phone was emitting a dial tone. He punched in a fourteen-digit number from memory, a number that belonged only to him and was to be used only in emergency circumstances. A series of clicking sounds and intermittent static indicated a sequence of satellite transfers, until a flat voice responded from Langley, Virginia.

"Satcom seven."

Ethan cleared his throat. "Central Europe. Unsecured."

"Designator?"

"Bravo Echo One One."

There was a delay of a few moments as the Langley operator checked a code on computer.

"Switching," said the flat voice.

What followed was another series of clicks and static bumps, and from the length of them Ethan knew his call was being bounced back through the network of satellites. Whoever he was being switched to was not in Langley. Finally, a tight, clipped voice responded. It belonged to a man Ethan knew of but had never met. Jim Phelps's boss at CIA.

"This is Kittridge."

Ethan instinctively rechecked his surroundings. A few kids smoking a joint ambled down the street, humming a halting version of an Alanis Morissette song. Ethan studied their movements and planned which one he would take out first if they approached him.

But they kept walking.

"Go secure," Ethan said to Kittridge.

Kittridge didn't answer, but Ethan heard a round of electronically jumbled sounds that meant the call was being relayed through a scrambling unit that would make the conversation, if monitored, sound like a digital aviary.

"Go ahead," Kittridge said again.

"They're dead."

"Who?"

"My team. Claire, Jack, Sarah, even Jim—Hannah, maybe, I—I don't know . . ."

"Are you damaged?"

"They knew we were coming," Ethan said bitterly. "Golitsyn's dead, too. The list is gone."

"Are you intact?" Kittridge inquired firmly.

"Do you read me?" Ethan breathed into the phone. "My team is dead. The list is in the open."

"I understand."

"And they damn well knew we were coming!"

"Let's just bring you in safely, and then we'll worry about that, okay? Were you followed from the scene?"

Kittridge sounded very much in control, concerned and reassuring.

Ethan took a deep breath. "I don't think so."

"Don't think, be certain. Are you clean?"

Ethan nodded. "Yes."

"Good. Location green. One hour. I'll be there myself."

"You're in Prague?"

There was a slight pause from Kittridge.

"Heard a lot about you, Hunt. Don't disappoint me."

"No, sir."

"One hour."

Kittridge clicked off. Ethan held the phone in his hands a few moments, staring at it. If the CIA's director of covert operations was in Prague, that told Ethan the embassy operation was red-line priority one. So where the hell was CIA backup? IMF mission or not, why would Kittridge risk Golitsyn's falling through the loop? He wouldn't. Hidden or not, there should have been redundant backup. Somewhere. Just in case.

He checked his watch. He had another hour of thinking to do.

Ethan found a street vendor in the student quarter and bought a jacket, T-shirt, rumpled pants, and a pair of running shoes. He changed in an alley and dumped the tuxedo in a trash bin. Then he walked toward location green, following the map that he had memorized earlier in the day.

Whenever he heard sirens, he dashed for cover and waited for the vehicles to pass. Two ambulances screamed past him, and it sickened him to think that the bodies of his friends might be inside.

Investigators were all over the crime scenes by now. The river was being dragged for the body of Jim Phelps. Detectives were dusting the knife that lay on the ground next to the bodies of Sarah and Golitsyn. Crime scene investigation technicians were trying to lift footprints from the wet pavement at the scene of the stabbing. Other technicians were gathering pieces of the BMW that had been scattered across the river walk. But Ethan knew that whatever the investigators found would be useless. Whoever killed Sarah and Golitsyn did so with swift efficiency. The car explosion had been potent and professional. No collateral damage—just the car and its contents. The bomb had been detonated at a particular moment when no pedestrians were nearby, no accidental killing of a diplomat's daughter that might cause an international incident. No, this was carefully done. Clues, if indeed there were any at all, would have been left intentionally, to misdirect the police. Jack Kiefer had been murdered inside the embassy by someone with access to very sophisticated electronics, equipment good enough to override Jack's own state-of-the-art stuff. Clean work, Ethan thought, planned, prepared, and carefully timed.

If Hannah were alive, she would find her way back to the safe house. The operative rule for any aborted mission was for the team to disperse instantly and reassemble at the safe house at the preplanned time, in this case 4 A.M. But Hannah had had plenty of time to walk from the embassy to the transport car. In all likelihood she'd been sitting in the car with Claire when the bomb went off. Ethan knew he could continue to hope Hannah was alive, but that was a stupid mind game, and the fact that he entertained it at all told him that he was vulnerable to the shock of death, IMF training notwithstanding. If Hannah was alive she would turn up at the safe house at 4 A.M., and Ethan would be there to meet her. It would, however, be a somber reunion.

He checked his watch and continued walking toward location green; no way would he take the chance of hailing a cab or riding public transportation. Given the level of compromise evidenced during the night's mission, there probably wasn't a square inch anywhere in Prague where Ethan would feel safe. He had to reach Kittridge, and only then would he be able to stop looking over his shoulder.

Despite location green's code name, it was simply a fancy restaurant built on the portico of an old Bohemian palace. Behind its glass a fake jungle bloomed; huge potted palms and ferns filled the spaces between aquariums and lobster tanks. Almost the entire front wall of the restaurant was one Herculean fish tank, a marvelous bit of engineering that was as good a sign as any that capitalism had firmly taken root in Prague. Of course, this restaurant was not built for locals. Much too expensive. It was built for tourists bearing American dollars, German marks, and credit cards of any kind.

Ethan pushed the doors open and entered the restaurant slowly, inspecting the clientele without staring at them. He picked up a book of matches from the lobby counter, buying more time to scan the room. It was training, and by now habit, for him to memorize the layout of a room upon entry. He checked doorways, stairs, curtains; he noted who sat with their back to a wall and who sat at the tables with the best views of the entire room. He noted who sat near an exit and who, if anyone, wasn't dressed appropriately for the surroundings. And all the while he was doing this, Ethan moved casually toward the center of the room, where Eugene Kittridge was dining alone. The smell of fine food nauseated Ethan at the moment, and the sight of diners eating their meals as if everything was right with the world unsettled him. Several of his colleagues and friends had just been slaughtered, and the images of their dying faces, and the shrieks from the torturous death suffered by Jack, burned in Ethan's brain. And even though Kittridge was here undercover, the sight of him zealously eating a lobster infuriated Ethan, though he maintained his practiced poker face as best he could.

As in the pictures Ethan had seen, Kittridge looked like a man accustomed to paperwork and committee meetings. He had the pallor of a bureaucrat but the confident, forceful eyes of a person used to wielding power. Kittridge seemed in no hurry, and in no particular distress. In fact, he appeared to be enjoying his lobster. When Ethan was a couple of yards away, Kittridge gestured toward the empty seat at his table, put his fork down, and stood to shake Ethan's hand.

"I can't tell you how sorry I am," he said quietly. "I know how much Jim in particular meant to you, Ethan. Personally as well as professionally."

Ethan took another quick scan of the room. "Yeah." Then he sat down.

Kittridge settled himself and went back to work on the lobster. Near Kittridge's wineglass, which contained only water, Ethan noticed a short stack of documents, and he reached for them. Among the papers were a Canadian passport with a photo of himself over the name Philippe Doucette, several credit cards, driver's license, and other identity papers.

"Passport, visa—you know the drill," Kittridge said, clearing away some empty shells. "We'll work the ex-filtration through Canada. Ottawa to Toronto to New York. Then Washington. We'll debrief at Langley. In the meantime, we'll toss the Prague police a bone, feed them a few suspects. Follow me?"

Ethan nodded. "I follow you," he said, his eyes finally locking in to Kittridge's.

Kittridge felt the stare, and let out a sigh. "We've lost enough agents for one night."

"You mean *I've* lost enough agents for one night."

About to speak, Kittridge paused, took a sip of water. He was choosing his words at this point with obvious care. "You seem to be blaming yourself for what happened tonight, Ethan."

"Well, who else is left?"

Kittridge flipped the lobster over and inspected its underside. Then he wrenched the tail off with a quick pop and crackle. "Yes," he said, "I see your point."

Ethan leaned forward and pushed the phony documents back to Kittridge's side of the table. "Why was there another team?"

Kittridge put his fork down. "What?"

"Of IMF agents. At the embassy. Tonight."

"I don't quite follow you."

"Then let's see if you can follow me around the room." Ethan turned and looked at the other diners. "The drunk Russians from the embankment outside the embassy are now sitting at seven and eight o'clock. The couple who waltzed me around the embassy are at nine and eleven. The waiter who was behind Hannah at the top of the staircase—bowtie, twelve o'clock. All here. Another IMF team. You're worried about me, Kittridge. Why?"

A tight little smile closing on his lips, Kittridge flicked his eyes around the room, then back at Ethan. Then he shrugged. "You're right, Hunt. Maybe this'll save some time."

Ethan saw that the others in the restaurant were restless now. Hands and feet shifted, positioning for a sudden move or a signal from Kittridge. But Kittridge gave a tiny hand gesture, motioning them all to stand down. He cleaned his hands in the fingerbowl and spent a long time drying his fingers with the napkin. Obviously, he was trying to sweat Ethan, make him wait. Prod him with indifference. But Ethan just sat there motionless, staring at Kittridge. Finally, Kittridge reached in his jacket and pulled out more documents.

"For a little over two years we've been spotting serious blowback in IMF operations," he said. "We have a penetration. The other day we decoded a message on the Internet from a Czech we know as Max."

Ethan nodded. "The arms dealer."

"That's right. Max, it seems, has two specific gifts: a capacity for anonymity and a talent for corrupting susceptible agents. This time he's gotten to someone on the inside. Way inside. He's put himself in position to buy our NOC list, an operation he referred to as 'job 314.' The job he thought Golitsyn was doing tonight."

"And the list Golitsyn stole tonight was a decoy," Ethan said, his face darkening.

"Of course. The actual list is safe at Langley. There is no outside access to the NOC list. Golitsyn was a lightning rod, one of ours."

"Another one of ours that is dead," Ethan said.

"Unfortunately, that's true."

"The cost of doing business," Ethan said, staring into Kittridge's eyes.

"I wouldn't use those exact words, but I suppose that's accurate."

Ethan leaned forward.

"This whole operation was a molehunt."

"Yes," Kittridge said, studying Ethan's increasingly dark demeanor. "The mole is deep inside. And, as you said, only you survived."

The two men continued to stare at each other for several seconds.

It should have been clear, Ethan thought, eyes locked into Kittridge's, the moment he heard that Golitsyn's target was the NOC list. It was too big, too tempting. Just the kind of thing to flush somebody into the open. A setup. Throw the players into the shark tank and see who swims safely to the surface. But this was not a game. Six people were dead, five of them Ethan's friends.

"My entire team is dead," Ethan said, his tone turning to ice, "for a molehunt."

Then Kittridge spoke again. "I want to show you something, Ethan," he said with a sneer, sliding the new papers across the table. Ethan glanced at them. They were photocopies of bank accounts. "Since your father's death, your family's farm has been in Chapter Eleven proceedings and now, suddenly, they're flush with over one hundred twenty-seven thousand dollars in an account held by your mother and uncle." Kittridge's tone deepened with righteous indignation, and disgust for Ethan Hunt. "Dad's illness had wiped out your mother's savings. Dying slowly in America is a very expensive proposition, I suppose. So why don't we go quietly out of here onto the plane?" By then Kittridge was practically spitting his words into Ethan's face.

Ethan trembled with anger. He slowly, imperceptibly lowered his right hand below the tablecloth, and into his pocket.

"How about if we just go quietly into the bathroom and I wash your mouth out with soap, you pathetic button-down bureaucratic asshole."

Kittridge made a feeble attempt at feigning concern. "I can understand that you're very upset."

"Kittridge," Ethan answered, controlling the fury that shook his body, "you've never seen me very upset."

Ethan slowly withdrew his hand from his pocket, but kept it out of sight.

Everything in the restaurant fell silent, except for the steady bubbling of the massive aquariums. In his peripheral vision, Ethan saw hands slide into jackets and toward hip holsters; he knew there was enough firepower surrounding him to blow a thousand holes in his back. Obviously, Kittridge knew it, too. And he did his best to stare Ethan down, again motioning with his fingers for the other agents in the room to hold steady. Then his mouth slid into a patronizing, tight sneer and he boldly leaned toward Ethan. "Hunt, you've bribed, cajoled, killed—and relied on intimate loyalties to get away with it. You're determined to shake hands with the devil and I'm going to make sure you do it in hell."

While Kittridge spoke, Ethan's right hand worked the stick of gum from the special pack that Jack had supplied him with. He silently counted the seconds as he mashed the green half of the gum into the red half.

Then, with blinding speed, Ethan swiped his left arm across the tabletop, sending water and wineglasses crashing into the air, and in the same motion whirled and fired the gum wad across the length of the restaurant. Kittridge jerked his head away from the diversion of the wineglasses and followed the trajectory of the gum, looking mystified as it splatted against the thick wall-length glass aquarium by the entryway. Suddenly, and too late to do anything about it, his eyes widened in recognition of what was about to happen.

The explosion shattered the entire front of the restaurant, sending hundreds of gallons of water roaring into the air, covering the agents and other diners with lobsters, seaweed, rocks, and fish. Tables went crashing over as people dove for cover. Chairs collapsed, trays crashed. And out from the middle of the debris Ethan sprang forward, bolting toward the plaza, smashing through shattering glass doors, followed by a thundering wall of water.

He sprinted across the plaza, disappearing into the fog before a single CIA agent could catch sight of him.

Eugene Kittridge was pulled to his feet by two backup agents, his ears ringing from the concussive blow of the explosion. All he could see when he looked at the gaping hole that was the front of the restaurant were darkness and fog and water.

Something that Jim Phelps had once said to him, when bragging about Ethan Hunt, came to mind. "If an agent as good as Ethan ever turned," Phelps had said jokingly, "you'd better hope I'm around to bring him in, because nobody else is going to be able to do it."

Safe House

ETHAN HUNT RAN ALONGSIDE THE VLTAVA RIVER, WHERE the fog completely obscured him from view. He reached an alley across the street from the safe house, and jerked open a Dumpster that was chained to a fence. Inside, right where it should be, he found a black box taped to the rear wall. The box had a keypad lock. Ethan punched in the combination, and pulled out a paging device that Jack Kiefer had stashed there as part of his safe house security preparation. The pager was linked to a motion detector inside the safe house that transmitted coded signals to the pager if there was any movement within the safe house after the mission leader—in this case, Phelps—abandoned his command post position. Following procedure, Phelps had activated the system when he raced to the embassy. Now, under Ethan's careful scrutiny, the pager indicated absolutely no activity in the safe house since Jim's departure hours ago.

The safe house location for an IMF mission was a piece of information kept on a need-to-know basis, meaning only the agents involved in the actual operation were privy to it. Phelps did not even let his bosses at Langley know the location; it was a policy that had worked for thirty years and one that had never changed. Still, given the evening's events, Ethan slipped into the building with great caution. Removing his jacket, he unscrewed the bare lightbulb at the top of the landing where the team's apartment was located. He crushed the bulb inside the jacket, then sprinkled glass on the top three steps, and repeated the procedure with the bulb just outside the door to the apartment.

Once inside, he charged into the living room, where the computer setup still glowed with blank screens. Ethan saw Jim's pack of Marlboros on the desktop, and the half dozen crushed butts in the ashtray. He grabbed a vase from the mantel, unscrewed its false base, and removed a Beretta 9mm semiautomatic, fourteen rounds in the clip. He chambered a round, then ran into the bathroom, where he unscrewed the false bottoms of shaving cream and hair spray cans, from which fell wads of money in dollars, marks, British pounds, francs, pesos, and Czech korunas. A plastic bottle of shampoo contained a Liechtenstein passport, properly credentialed to Ethan. With this stash of credentials and cash he could operate with a high level of efficiency for a month; additionally, the IMF kept three bank accounts, authorized by, but secret from, the CIA for use in procuring equipment and bribes in emergency situations. Again, Phelps had maintained these accounts for thirty years and refused to change procedures for Kittridge or the CIA. As far as Ethan knew, he and Phelps were the only IMF operatives with the codes to the accounts. But after what he saw take place at the embassy tonight, Ethan wondered if even these emergency accounts would be accessible.

He splashed water on his face, rinsed dirt and Sarah Norman's dried blood from his hands, then took a look in the mirror. Exhausted, running on pure adrenaline, he saw that every muscle in his face was taut. Seeing his own features reminded him of his family, and he continued to seethe at Kittridge for having invoked the names of his mother and uncle, and daring to speak of his father's death. It had taken every ounce of Ethan's professionalism and training to prevent him from reaching across that restaurant table and ripping Kittridge's larynx right out of his throat. Even so, he found it hard to believe that a man of Kittridge's experience would seriously entertain the notion that an IMF agent with Ethan's decorated background would compromise his family, colleagues, and integrity, all for a paltry one hundred and twenty-seven thousand dollars in his mother's bank account. Yet Kittridge had spent years dealing with the fallout from the CIA's Aldrich Ames scandal, when U.S. military and intelligence secrets of the highest sensitivity were sold to the Soviets just so Ames could live in a nicer home and drive a Jaguar. The price of treason, certainly in that case, turned out to be embarrassingly modest. No doubt Kittridge believed Ethan had stashed millions in dirty money someplace. Or maybe Kittridge had discovered the secret IMF accounts and thought Ethan was looting them. Did Kittridge truly believe Ethan would sacrifice the lives of Jim and Claire Phelps for money?

And though Ethan Hunt knew he was not the mole Kittridge was looking for, he was still haunted by his decision to ignore Jim Phelps's abort instruction.

All of those lives lost for a molehunt? An unsuccessful molehunt, at that. He believed he made the correct decision to pursue Golitsyn against Jim's order, given what he thought were the stakes of Golitsyn's theft. But it was hard to feel right about it at this moment.

Ethan walked into the kitchen, jerked three bottles of mineral water from the refrigerator, and poured them down his throat as quickly as he could. He grabbed two of Claire's protein-rich Powerbars, tore the wrappers off, and shoved them into his mouth.

He stood there chewing, not tasting but trying to fuel his body against growing fatigue. His mind raced. He wondered if Jim had called the abort simply because Jack went down, or was it the fact that his own wife, Claire, might be in jeopardy? Didn't he know that Ethan would give his own life to protect her or any other member of the team? If Jim had stayed in the command post, could he have warned Sarah of the attacker who eventually killed her and Golitsyn? Ethan knew he would be turning these questions over in his mind for the rest of the night, and possibly for the rest of his life. But he had to focus. He had to form his own plan, and quickly, because Kittridge would have the special surveillance and search team from Vienna already in Prague conducting a grid-and-sector search, complemented by entire teams of European CIA operatives and agents; soon Prague would become a very small city to hide in.

But hiding, Ethan decided, would not be his objective. He wanted to know who had outmaneuvered two teams of IMF agents and the entire CIA, even if it was only to obtain a phony NOC list.

Ethan knew he wasn't the mole who originated job "314" with Max the arms dealer. But Max had to know who that person was. So he had to get to Max.

Pushing aside the stale-smelling cigarette butts, Ethan dropped to a chair in front of the computer setup.

On the screen that windowed the Visco transmissions he saw black-outlined boxes with the names of each team member below them. He looked at Claire's name. That's what was left of her: a name with static above it. Ethan felt a chill shoot through his body. The team was dead, but the computers hummed along. Welcome to espionage work in the nineties.

Ethan expelled a deep sigh and began typing into one of the Apple Powerbook computers. He brought up an Internet navigator that inquired of him:

select usenet group

Ethan thought about what to do next, then typed:

job 314

and launched the search. A few moments later:

searching string not found

He shrugged, mumbling to himself, "Job. Job, three-fourteen. March fourteen. Job thirty-one. Job thirty-one, four. April." He tried various combinations. No luck. Then:

max.com.

Again the search string came up empty. He then focused on "job" and tried "job," "jobs," "joblist.com." The same prompt reappeared:

searching string not found

Time to change tactics. He typed:

scroll usenet groups

This command produced an avalanche of short titles that zoomed down the screen much too quickly to follow. Hundreds and hundreds of them. This could take forever.

He sat back in his chair and rubbed his eyes. Then he looked again at the sophisticated computer setup on the disk. And he realized that even though Kittridge didn't know the location of the safe house, if the CIA had set up a molehunt at the embassy, certainly they'd flown in enough gadgetry from Langley that they could be pinpointing this setup right now. Kittridge could have a team of his best cyber ops hacking into every communications relay station in Eastern Europe in an attempt to link into Ethan's computer activity. And Kittridge knew damn well that Ethan would be looking for Max and trying to shake loose more information about job 314, which had brought about the death of his team. Maybe Kittridge had already cracked Jack's Visco frequency codes and traced them to this setup. And if he had, why was he leaving Ethan here all by himself? Maybe it was because Kittridge wanted him to look for Max, Ethan speculated. The molehunt had been a failure, after all, so why not use Ethan to find Max? No doubt Kittridge couldn't find Max himself. He's leaving it up to me, Ethan concluded.

Looking at the hundreds of usenet groups that continued to scroll across the screen, Ethan also decided that Kittridge might have one hell of a wait on his hands.

Job three-fourteen, he forced himself to think. J is the tenth letter of the alphabet, O is the fifteenth, B the second. Ten, fifteen, two. Adds up to twenty-seven. Twenty-seven plus three plus fourteen equals forty-four.

He tapped at the computer.

search job 44

The computer searched unsuccessfully.

He knew he could play this game for days. If he had a sequencer he could try every numerical combination possible. But it would take a couple of days, at least, to obtain a quality sequencer. He stood and paced around the room, repeating the word "job." Ethan stopped and stared out the window, polished off another bottle of mineral water, then tossed it at the bookshelf in front of him. Dozens and dozens of books in half a dozen different languages. At least, whoever had this apartment before the IMF was well read. Then his eyes fell on one title, this one in English. It was the Holy Bible, and a thought bubbled up in his brain. He looked at the word "job" on his computer screen and thought of the biblical pronunciation. "Job," he said aloud. "Job." He snatched the Gideon Bible off the shelf and opened to the Book of Job in the Old Testament. "Chapter three, verse fourteen. Book of Job." It was a passage that began "Kings and counselors . . ."

He dropped to the computer desk again and typed:

Bible

The computer replied: -

126 entries found/specify group

He typed:

Book of Job

The computer screen turned light blue and displayed a batch of religious-themed icons: lambs, stars, saints with halos, crucifixes, Stars of David, and an open Bible. A message window opened:

Welcome to the Book of Job discussion group. Which chapter and verse do you wish to post your message under?

Ethan carefully entered "Job 3:14" and was instantly greeted with an open message box and a request to post text. He considered his words, then started typing:

Max—goods tainted.
Consider extremely hazardous.
DO NOT USE. Fate will be that of kings and counselors who built for themselves palaces now lying in ruins. Must meet to discuss a.s.a.p.

Ethan knew that he might be sending this message into oblivion, but it was his best guess and, at this point, his only one; he pushed the send key. The screen asked if he wanted to send another message. He did not.

He sat back in the chair, closed his eyes, and waited, feeling the tension in his neck and back muscles, and the aching in his legs from having sprinted all over Prague. Sleep would be wonderful, but he couldn't risk it. Yet staying awake was its own nightmare, because every second he was awake he tortured himself about defying Jim's order to abort. He'd been making serious judgment calls his entire life. Bachelor's degree from Wisconsin State University, master's from Princeton, FBI training, CIA training, special tactics and forces training, special weapons training, advanced linguistics and electronics. Ethan knew his judgment calls were not pulled out of thin air. They were based on solid training and field experience, not to mention the stability of a strong family background.

He'd grown up on a farm not far from Madison, Wisconsin, the only child of devoted parents who recognized early on that their son was exceedingly bright. Ethan's father did not want the instability of a farmer's lot in the modern age for his son. The Hunts used every penny of their disposable income to see that Ethan received the best education available. He earned straight A's all through high school, and was offered numerous scholarships both for academics and as a nationally ranked gymnast. His father hoped Ethan's early years in the CIA were simply a training ground for a career as a diplomat, or perhaps a cabinet post. But just at the time Ethan became disenchanted with the petty politics of government bureaucracies, Jim Phelps had come into his life.

Jim not only encouraged his people to take charge, to assume the responsibilities of sudden, necessary changes of plan, he demanded it. That's what separated IMF operations from CIA or any other covert operation. IMF agents were prepared and equipped to go it alone. There was no such thing as politically correct behavior in their world, no advancement for being a yes man. However, an abort signal from Phelps was not something IMF team members would generally question. In fact, probably only Ethan Hunt, considered the IMF's top agent, would readily challenge it.

Ethan wondered whether, had Phelps never allowed himself and the IMF to be folded into the CIA's covert wing, perhaps a disaster like this one might never have happened. Jim Phelps seemed more cautious once he started working for Eugene Kittridge and the CIA. And sometimes being overly cautious led to mistakes. Perhaps he had to be too concerned with the political backlash of missions; maybe Jim even had aspirations of becoming the CIA director, and therefore wanted to make the moves to ensure that eventuality. Maybe he called the abort so that the CIA would have to take the blame for the mission, rather than having it play out as an IMF failure.

Or, Ethan considered, maybe it wasn't any of that. Maybe it was all about Claire.

After all, before marrying Claire, Jim simply didn't

make mistakes. In the five years that Ethan had worked for the IMF he recalled having one or two serious arguments with Jim about the planning or executions of missions. Things rarely went wrong. But since marrying Claire, Jim had turned down an increasing number of missions, and he'd grown testy about having his plans challenged by Ethan. There had been a few recent flare-ups in missions, causing a slight rift between Ethan and Jim. Ethan wanted final word on all missions on which he was point man. Jim said the CIA had final word. That was the way things worked. Still, Ethan ignored CIA directives he didn't approve of. Maybe Jim had been testing him tonight, maybe he gave the abort signal to reassert his authority over Ethan's team. But he wouldn't do that, Ethan reminded himself. Jim would not carelessly risk lives. Not his own, especially not Claire's. But the thoughts continued to roil in Ethan's brain. He was simply unable to accept that the mission could have gone so wrong. And for the first time during his tenure at the IMF Ethan thought it was time to leave. Not just leave the IMF but leave the covert world altogether. Ethan's father had died six years ago, without knowing what final career path his son would take. And his mother, along with her brother Donald, ran the family farm, barely keeping it afloat. Maybe this was the time for Ethan to use his brains to revitalize the farm his father had loved. A simpler life. That sounded appealing at this moment. Anything to keep from hearing Jack's screams, or from seeing the image of a bullet hole in the chest of Jim Phelps, or the memory of kneeling over Sarah as life drained from her helpless eyes.

And Claire. Three days ago in Kiev he'd held her head in his hands, and stuck a needle in her that, like magic, had brought her back to consciousness. She had put her life in his hands on so many occasions. But last night's mission was different. This time she died. Claire Phelps, like the rest of the team, was now nothing more than a silent transmission of static on a computer screen.

After what he thought had been only seconds, Ethan opened his eyes again. The computer's screen had not changed. Fatigue weighed upon his eyelids, but he willed it away. To close his eyes meant images from the evening rushed in front of him in nightmare fashion, all played out in torturous slow motion. Screams, blood, the car with Claire inside exploding, flying into the air like a tossed toy.

And Kittridge eating the lobster. Chewing it right in Ethan's face while he talked about dead members of the IMF team. Cracking shells while telling Ethan he was sorry about Jim and the others, believing as he ate that Ethan was a mole. An obvious mole, at that, funneling dirty money to bail out his mother's farm from Chapter Eleven proceedings. There had been that look in Kittridge's eyes that silently asked where the big money might be hidden, the millions that Ethan had probably stashed in the name of a phony business in a Cayman Islands bank. Kittridge had looked at him with an expression that said, "You may be good, but now we've got you." There were dead members of Ethan's IMF team strewn about the streets near Prague's American embassy, and yet Kittridge could sit in that restaurant and enjoy a lobster, intending for the very casual nature of the act to be a message to Ethan that the game was over. Ethan had been flushed out, to be processed with the rest of the garbage, and the lives of those other IMF agents were simply the cost of exposing the mole, the cost of doing business in a cold, hard world.

A crunching sound snapped Ethan's head toward the doorway.

He whirled in time to see Jim Phelps stagger into the apartment, wet and muddy, a gaping bloody wound in his chest.

Ethan froze, stunned.

Pale, coughing up water and blood, Phelps staggered forward like he wanted to die at Ethan's feet.

"Ethan, what are you doing?" Phelps gasped, lurching to put his hand on Ethan's shoulder.

Ethan couldn't speak.

"I needed you, Ethan," Jim said. "I needed you on the bridge, and—you weren't there. Ethan? Ethan?"

Ethan tried to grab Phelps, keep him from falling, but his arms passed right through Jim Phelps, and suddenly Phelps wasn't there at all. But somebody was standing there.

Leaping to his feet, Ethan spun away from the shadowy figure, grabbed his Beretta, and dropped into a firing stance.

And as the hallucination of Jim Phelps crashed away in a hazy blur, he found himself lining the titanium sights of his gun onto the approaching figure of . . . Claire Phelps.

Her hair was matted, face drawn with shock and fatigue, clothes scuffed and stained. But it was Claire, alive and staring at Ethan and the black barrel of his gun. She slowly raised a hand, palm open, seeing the dazed, confused, paranoid look on his face, afraid that he might pull the trigger.

"What are you doing here?!" were the words that spilled out of Ethan's mouth.

Claire carefully raised her other hand, to show Ethan she carried no weapons.

"Ethan," she said, forcing a calm tone into her shaken voice, "it's okay. It's Claire." She watched him and lowered her hands a bit.

"Don't move," he spit at her, reacting to the tiniest movement of her hands.

"Ethan, what's wrong with you?"

He kept the pistol aimed at the bridge of her nose. Claire froze.

"You were in the car," he said, circling in closer to her, his eyes wide and wild.

She shook her head slowly, trying to keep his eyes engaged, while he checked the hallway behind her, poked his head out and scanned the entry area for accomplices.

"I wasn't," Claire said. "I heard on the radio that Jim was in trouble. He said someone was . . ."

"Shut up! I saw you. You were in the car."

"No," she answered, with precision that came from rigorous IMF hostage and interrogation training, her voice firm but not argumentative. "I got out of the car, and I ran to the bridge. Hannah was in the car."

"I was on the bridge, Claire. I was standing there. I saw no one."

She closed her eyes a moment. "What happened to Jim?"

Ethan lunged forward until his face was just inches

from hers, like he still didn't believe she was a breathing, living human being.

"Dead. Dead! Wake up, Claire! Jim's dead, they're dead. They are all dead."

"Jim's dead," she said simply, looking away from Ethan for the first time, as if she suspected this would be the news, but it was not reality to her until she heard it from Ethan.

"Yes, and the others." He kept the gun on her.

"They're dead?" she mumbled, tears starting to slide from her eyes. "Jim's dead?"

Ethan circled back around in front of her, his features distorted in a way Claire had never seen.

"Take off your coat," Ethan ordered.

"What?"

"Take off your goddamned coat!" he bellowed, grabbing one of her sleeves and tearing the coat off of her, spinning her around.

She shivered, covering her chest with her arms.

"Where were you?" he demanded, running a hand over her body, checking for concealed weapons or a transmitter.

"I walked away," Claire said. "I started for the bridge. Jim called abort. And then he was gone so I walked away. I never saw what happened."

"That was it, you just walked away," he said derisively, continuing to search her.

"And the car exploded, but I kept going. I followed orders. He called abort." Her face was streaked with tears and her voice rose with intensity.

Ethan's weary mind raced as he listened to Claire's story, looking for flaws. He looked at her, happy she was alive, though paranoid about her sudden presence. What she had just described made sense to him; she had described proper procedure, but somehow, in his agitated state, it sounded too simple.

"That was four hours ago," Ethan said. "Who sent you? Are you wired?"

He finished patting her down.

"No," she said.

"Did they send you here?"

"Who are 'they'?" she asked very slowly, looking in his eyes, having had enough of this interrogation.

Ethan grabbed her by the wrists. "Who sent you? Tell me right now who sent you!"

"No one sent me!" she screamed in his face. "We're supposed to be back here at four o'clock if we abort, four o'clock, we don't return here until four o'clock, oh–four hundred, four A.M., Ethan, four o'clock." The words came spitting out of her mouth, as she tried to break away from the grip he had on her wrists.

Then she let out a deep breath as somewhere in Prague a bell chimed, a deep, plaintive sound that resonated on the empty stone streets.

The awareness came over Ethan's face that the bell chimed four times. Four A.M. The precise time of the designated return to the safe house in case of an abort. Which was exactly what Claire was trying to tell him. She was still following procedure. He had not. He had ignored the abort order and he had come here early, following his confrontation with Kittridge.

"Four o'clock," she whispered, seeing that he was beginning to calm, letting his guard down.

And his face changed. Claire saw recognition and resignation come into his eyes, as he gradually released her wrists and drew her close to him.

"Four o'clock," he whispered back to her, a hollow sadness in his voice.

They embraced in the awful silence of the safe house, only the hum of the computers buzzing in the room. He held her close, desperate for answers, thankful that Claire had survived, thankful that he was not alone. Ethan felt Claire's body trembling; she was cold and the tears continued to fall from her eyes.

"Claire," he said, his voice quiet as a breath.

"What happened?" she asked, her words barely audible.

"I don't know yet," he answered.

"My God, Ethan," she said, as reality set in deeper and deeper.

"Claire," he said again, still holding her limp body.

The city was completely peaceful just before dawn. Ethan sat in front of the computer, hoping for a response from Max. Claire sat on a couch, rubbing her forehead, thinking. She had asked him to recount every detail of the mission and its aftermath. She wanted details of Jim's shooting, of Sarah's murder, and what happened with the car. Ethan replayed his decision to ignore the abort and pursue Golitsyn, and in doing so he searched Claire's face for signals as to whether she held him responsible for what happened. But he found her to be just as unrevealing as himself.

After a long silence, she asked, "Why haven't they brought us in yet?"

"I've been disavowed. They think I killed Jim and everyone else. You included. Somehow one hundred twenty-seven thousand dollars found its way into my family's bank account. Kittridge assumes I'm a mole

91

they've been tracing and that I've been in the employ of an arms dealer, Max, for the last two years, to get him our NOC list."

She let all of that sink in, turning it over piece by piece. Then, "What are you going to do?"

"I'm going to get it for him," he answered steadily, having been thinking about this for the past two hours while he recounted the night's events to Claire. "Whoever the mole is, I think he goes by the name of Job, at least part of the time. I can't find him, but if Job knows I have the NOC list, he'll find me."

"Ethan, you're not making sense. Why don't I just go in to Kittridge? I'm going to tell him you had nothing to do with—"

"Claire," he said, cutting her off. "We're way past that. Think about it. If you're not dead, Kittridge is going to assume you're with me in all of this."

She started to speak, but the computer emitted a small beep, signaling incoming e-mail.

Both of them snapped their eyes to the screen.

A "Message Waiting" prompt pulsed in front of them.

Ethan move the cursor to the message box and clicked. The screen blinked and up popped the following:

?	JOB—CORNER OF NEKAZANKA AND PRIKOPY ONE P.M.
?	BUY A PACKET OF DUNHILL
?	AND ASK THE MAN SITTING ON THE BUS
?	STOP BENCH FOR A MATCH

Claire leaned over Ethan's shoulder and read the message, then looked at him.

"The message is for Job," she said, realizing its implications.

Ethan nodded. "I'm going to answer it."

Max

ETHAN LOGGED TWO FITFUL HOURS OF SLEEP, THEN LEFT
the safe house at nine-thirty, disguised as a pros-
perous businessman, complete with briefcase and
Russian hat. Max had a reputation for professional
tradecraft suggesting a degree of strong intelligence
training, so Ethan initiated his own precise countermeasures. He found a coffeeshop half a block away
from the bus stop rendezvous area. Ethan sat there for
two and a half hours, sipping coffee and hiding behind
newspapers, all the while observing the newsstand,
checking to see if anyone dropped packages of any
kind in the trash receptacle next to the bench; he
scanned surrounding buildings for any unusual activity in the windows, such as placement of listening
cones. Ethan unobtrusively worked his way to the roof
of the tallest building on the street and from there
scouted other rooftops for listening posts and snipers.

He mentally logged the cars that parked on the street, noting vans, trucks, or any vehicles that could conceal people. By the time 1 P.M. came around, Ethan felt confident he was not walking into a trap. At least, not an obvious one.

He bought a pack of Dunhill's, and wondered if Max intended any subtle message by requiring him to buy the most expensive cigarettes in the world. Then he eyeballed the man sitting on the bus stop bench. Long hair, pale complexion, and fierce eyes that never once turned to look at Ethan or anyone else. This was not a casual citizen.

Ethan cautiously approached him, sliding up from behind with ghostlike silence. "Excuse me, could I trouble you for a match?"

Without turning to look at Ethan, the man offered up a box of matches. And as he did, a large Mercedes sedan with Czech plates slid through the traffic and stopped precisely in front of the bus stop. Another man materialized from somewhere to push Ethan into the rear seat of the sedan, where he was flanked by two men.

In the front seat, a dark, well-dressed man sat staring straight ahead; he never bothered to look at Ethan.

Next to Ethan, Matthias, a long-haired German man with fierce blue eyes, held up a black hood. He extended it to Ethan, who made no move to take it.

"Would you remove your hat, please?" Matthias said in a voice that expected compliance.

"Why?"

"You wish to meet Max? This is the price of

admission. Considering the one hundred and twenty-seven thousand dollars we paid you earlier, this price is not so much to ask, is it?"

Reluctantly, Ethan nodded, and Matthias pushed the hood over Ethan's head and cinched it tight, then the Mercedes took off at a high rate of speed. From the smell inside the hood, Ethan knew he was not its first occupant, and he hoped the ride would be brief. As the car worked through traffic, Ethan heard the electric hum of a radio frequency scanner passing over his body as the men checked for transmitters and recording devices. Matthias mumbled something to the driver and the car took a hard right turn, then another, then a series of turns and stops designed to make absolutely certain, just in case Ethan had a map of Prague embedded in his brain, that he couldn't retrace this route. This was a wise move on their part, since Ethan had committed to memory the layout of streets within an eight-block radius of the rendezvous location.

Fifteen minutes later, hood still in place, Ethan was hustled from the car and up a stairway. He discerned from the sounds that the stairway was wide and made of very fine wood. This was no cheap apartment or industrial building. When he was pushed down in a chair he instantly knew it was a fine piece of furniture, and from the bounce of the voices in the room he guessed it was a twenty-foot ceiling with stucco curves in the corners. A nice place, he assumed. He lifted his hands to the armrests and let the exposed flesh of his fingers feel for airflow; in case of the sudden need for escape, he wanted to know window locations and whether they were open. He listened for traffic to determine the kind of neighborhood they were in. It was very quiet here, broken only by the rhythmic barking of a dog about half a block away. From the walk up the stairs Ethan knew he was on the third floor. He listened for the subtlest sounds of the people in the room, and used them to mark their locations, creating a mental image of the room and its inhabitants. More than once in his career he had used this sensory training to escape dangerous situations.

"I thought I was going to see Max," Ethan said at last.

"You misunderstood," came the reply. "No one sees Max."

"Then what am I doing here?"

"Allowing Max to see you and hear what you've got to say," Matthias answered.

"I don't communicate very well through a shroud."

"Yes, well, if Max doesn't like what you have to say, the shroud becomes permanent."

"I'm willing to take that chance," Ethan said steadily.

There was a silence, during which, Ethan assumed, Max was making his decision. For all Ethan knew, Matthias was Max and had been assessing him all along.

Suddenly the hood was jerked off his head, and Ethan found himself squinting at Max, a tall woman in her fifties, tastefully dressed and groomed, handsome to the point of severity.

"Who are you and what are you doing here?" she asked, by way of a greeting.

"I need one hundred thousand dollars," Ethan said brightly.

"Really?" Max answered, looking quizzically at her three associates in the room. "And you thought if you simply showed up I might give it to you?"

"Why not?" Ethan said. "You gave Job a hundred and twenty-seven thousand."

His eyes quickly took in the room. Pretty much as he had constructed it from his nonsighted analysis. The dog down the street continued to bark with the regularity of a metronome.

"The penny drops," Max said. "You, I am to understand, are not Job. Yes, Job is not given to quoting scripture in his communications. And there was its tone—aggressive but playful. Job is not playful. So you're something of a paradox."

"That depends."

"On what?"

"Whether you like a paradox. I now want a hundred and fifty thousand dollars."

"It's quite out of the question," Max said.

"The disk Job sold you is worthless. It's bait, part of an internal molehunt."

"I see," she said, slightly less patient than she was a moment ago. She looked at her colleagues. They were annoyed. "And how might you know that? Are you another company man?"

"Like Job?"

"We're asking about you."

"I'm NOC. Was. Now disavowed."

"Why, may I ask?"

"That's the question I want to ask Job," Ethan replied, meeting Max's stare.

"I don't know Job any more than he knows me," she told him.

"Even so, I'm sure you could arrange an introduction."

"Why should I?"

"Because I can deliver the actual NOC list. The one you picked up last night is not only worthless, it's certain to be equipped with a homing device to pinpoint your exact location."

She spread her hands in a gesture of futility. "It's easy to say the disk is worthless when you say I can't even look at the information and *see* if it's worthless without setting off a homing device. Not a tenable position, sir."

Ethan stood and stretched, eliciting a quick reaction from the bodyguards flanking him. But Ethan didn't mind. He looked out the window and let out a sigh, then turned toward Max and gave her a look like the one she'd given him, one of increasing frustration. "Okay, boot up the disk and in anywhere from thirty seconds to ten minutes you're gonna have Virginia farm boys hopping around you like jackrabbits."

Max studied Ethan.

"I don't know," she said, looking out the window, thinking.

"Tell you what," Ethan said helpfully. "How good is the radio frequency scanner this gentleman used in the car?"

"Very good. State of the art."

"Okay, use it. But I suggest you pack up first."

Max smiled. She'd been in more high-stakes poker games than most. And she usually won.

"Very good," she said, pulling an acrylic diskette case from her desk. The case still had bloodstains on it. She handed it to Matthias, who slipped it into the desktop PC adjacent to where Max was sitting. He booted the disk, and at the same time checked the digital readout on the RF scanner. The scanner carefully measured the levels of electronic signals in the room, and as long as the readout stayed below 30, there was no activity other than the usual emissions from the computer. A homing signal triggered from the disk would send the readout climbing.

The computer screen blinked on, and a chirping sound indicated the disk was being accessed. The screen filled with names, addresses, phone numbers, and other personal information. All of which looked like very good news to Max.

Matthias kept an eye on the scanner.

"Twenty-six, twenty-seven," he read aloud. "So far so good."

"But not so good for our friend here," Max said, looking directly at Ethan.

A few more seconds went by. "Thirty-two and changing," Matthias said, glancing up at Max.

"Doesn't mean it's a signal," she said. "Could just be the hard drive heating up."

"Forty-four, forty-five."

Max looked at the scanner, then at Ethan, studying his face.

He knew what she was thinking. "I'd say you've got about two minutes," he told her.

One of the other men went to the balcony off the French doors. He looked down the street in both directions. Nothing but a beautiful afternoon and the incessant barking of the dog.

Then the dog abruptly stopped barking.

Kittridge, Ethan thought, the moment the dog ceased its barking.

"Fifty-seven," Matthias said, his voice growing edgy. "Fifty-nine."

Ethan looked calmly at Max. At that moment he knew that she now trusted what he had told her.

A white pollution control van and a taxi arrived simultaneously on the street below. Kittridge and a female agent exited the taxi. Several agents dressed in coveralls, carrying what was supposed to look like cleaning equipment, climbed out of the van and headed for the building.

"Van and taxi outside," the man from the balcony said. "Half dozen people entering, some kind of cleaning service."

Max emitted a small smile.

Ethan shrugged and looked at his watch, assuming that Kittridge's team would be following a tech op who was checking a scanner and pointing to the stairs.

Ethan was correct.

Once in the building's lobby, the CIA team in coveralls opened hollow shop-vac canisters and withdrew weapons from them.

When they reached the landing of the floor where Max's apartment was, they were met by a cleaning woman who was vacuuming the hallway. The woman saw the weapons, flicked off her vacuum, and started backing up.

101

Ethan heard the vacuum turn off outside the apartment. He gave Max a look that said, They're here.

Out in the hallway, a female CIA agent quickly approached the cleaning woman, pointed to the vacuum, and in Czech ordered, "Switch it back on."

The trembling cleaning woman obeyed, while the tech op pointed to a door. Kittridge signaled his bomb expert to sweep the doorway. That done, two other agents kicked the door in and the team poured into the apartment, moving in pairs to sweep each room. Kittridge followed the assault team inside. But all they found was a large, well-decorated apartment that smelled like cigarettes.

"Two minutes ago," Kittridge said to his second-in-command, a tweedy-looking man named Harry Barnes who didn't particularly like his boss. "Maybe one minute, and we would have had them."

"Traffic," Barnes said.

The team had picked up the signal loud and clear just three and a half minutes ago, and their global positioning device had given them the good news that the homing diskette was less than a mile from their position. But the traffic had been snarled on two of the necessary side streets. All the technology in the world couldn't outflank an angry Czech cabdriver who'd left his cab dead in the street while he chased a nonpaying customer around the corner. And by saying "traffic" to Kittridge, Harry Barnes was purposely irritating his boss. Barnes enjoyed knocking Kittridge off his perch now and then.

While the two CIA men talked, Max and Ethan followed Matthias and Max's team across an enclosed bridge that connected the apartment building where they'd just been with another building. From there, they rushed downstairs to the waiting Mercedes.

"The man's gone black," Kittridge said to Barnes, of Ethan Hunt. "He's under until he decides to surface."

"We can use someone from the embassy and we can get the local authorities more involved," Barnes suggested. "Close off his transportation."

"What can we do, Barnes? Put a guy at the airport? Sure. How many identities do you think Hunt has? How many times has he slipped past customs, in how many countries? These guys are trained to be ghosts. *We* taught them how to do it, for Christ's sake, and then Jim Phelps perfected it. Hell, Phelps taught us things about disappearing that we hadn't even thought of. And Phelps told me that Hunt taught him a few things that he, in turn, would never have thought of. So what do you think our chances are of pulling in Ethan Hunt?"

"Well, what do you suggest?" Barnes said, laying the matter right back on Kittridge's doorstep.

"Let's not waste any time chasing him," Kittridge said, walking out to the balcony and looking at the deserted street below. "Make him come to us. Everybody's got pressure points. Find out something that's important to him personally and you squeeze."

"How's he even going to know? He may drop off the face of the earth. Let things cool down."

"Then we keep squeezing until the pain is so intense we'll hear Hunt's scream all the way from Langley. In the meantime, I want our people to visit every apartment in this building, search them all, and see who remembers anything about the people here."

Barnes nodded, knowing it was going to be a long, unpleasant flight back to Washington.

"And I wish somebody would shut that damn dog up," Kittridge added.

Three blocks from the building and gaining speed, Max's Mercedes deftly moved through traffic. This time Ethan was in the rear seat with Max. Matthias was in front with the driver. The rest of Max's team was in another, identical, car, taking an entirely different route, protecting against the unlikely event that they'd been spotted fleeing the area.

Ethan had been impressed with the efficiency of Max's sudden evacuation from the apartment. An escape route had been planned and the exit procedures followed with precision. No doubt these people had made dozens of quick exits in the past. And there was also no doubt in Ethan's mind that at this very moment Kittridge was back in the apartment, ripping it apart for clues.

"Dear," Max said, "I'm sure Gunther will never let me use one of his apartments again. I'm sure your people won't leave it in the tidiest condition." She put a hand over Ethan's. "Sorry I doubted you, dear boy. You're a good sport. Do accept the compliment."

"Thanks, Max. Or is it Maxine?"

"Does it matter? I don't have to tell you what a comfort anonymity can be in my profession. Like a warm blanket." She shifted to face him. "My deal with Job was subject to a successful boot scan. Obviously, it didn't pass muster. Deal's off."

"What was your deal with Job?"

"Reasonable, I thought. Six million dollars." She let the large sum float in the air and settle in with Ethan. Then she continued. "I'll give you the same. But I want the complete list now, not just Eastern Europe. I won't do this piecemeal, it's too time-consuming, not to mention dangerous. I want the entire list, the true name of every nonofficial cover agent throughout the world. There it is."

"Well, good luck to you," Ethan said, turning his attention to the passing scenery.

"Not interested?"

"Not for six million dollars."

"My dear boy, you risked your life today in order to meet, without a guarantee of one cent. Obviously, your motivation for doing business with me runs deeper than pure economic gain. Or do you assume I'm stupid?"

"I assume you'll pay what is necessary to get what you want," Ethan said, "and in this case it is ten million dollars."

"I see."

"Ten million in negotiable U.S. Treasury certificates, in bearer form, coupons attached."

"Oh."

"And one more thing. Your personal assurance that Job will be at the exchange."

She stared straight ahead. "Done. Bring it to me in London. I want it by the end of the week. Those are my terms."

"How will you make certain Job will be there?"

"How will you make sure I'll have the list in three

days?" She smiled at him. "It's been a delight. But no doubt you have much to do. So, where can I drop you?"

Ethan shook his head. "I'm not being dropped anywhere without my money."

"What, the hundred fifty thousand?"

"That's correct."

"I don't see where it's my responsibility to finance your operation. Particularly since we just met."

"You trust me, don't you, Max?"

"I'm certain there's no question about that," she said. Her eyes took in the traffic up ahead. She came to her decision quickly. "I'm going to front you personally. Don't lose that money without losing your life."

"I wouldn't dream of it."

"All right," she said to Matthias. "Let's visit the banker."

Matthias mumbled something in Czech to the driver, who veered across lanes and took the next left.

Max settled back in her seat and regarded Ethan. She let out a theatrical sigh. He was taking up a great deal of her time. Fortunately, she liked him.

When Ethan returned to the safe house, Claire was waiting in the dining room, having dismantled the electronics setup, tossed out accumulated garbage, scrubbed the place of prints and remaining personal items. She had a Glock 9 pistol stuck in her belt.

He put a zippered case on the table and opened it to reveal the bundles of currency.

"Max made a deal with you?" she said.

"I deliver the NOC list, Max delivers Job," he said, with typical IMF brevity, except in this situation he was talking about exposing the person responsible for Jim Phelps's death, and for framing Ethan as part of the deal. For Claire, it meant pinpointing the killer of her husband—not a typical IMF assignment.

Ethan saw the same thoughts flash through Claire's eyes, then she got down to business. "We've got seventy-five rounds for the Glock, twenty-eight for the Beretta, one pair of functioning Visco glasses with monitor, plenty of passports."

"Claire, you—"

She cut him off. "You said it yourself, Ethan. If I'm not dead, I'm with you."

"You could find a safe house in London and wait it out."

"Wait what out, Ethan? You plan to take on Max, Job, Kittridge, and the CIA by yourself? I'm in."

"You're sure about this?"

"I don't have a point to prove. But I do want the son of a bitch who killed my husband."

He nodded as they exchanged looks. Ethan regarded Jim as a second father. He knew it, and Claire knew it. And considering the feelings he had for Claire, he just didn't want to approach the subject right at the moment. But they were already there. And he didn't want to see Claire killed because Kittridge was locking in on Ethan as his mole.

"The decision is made, Ethan," Claire said, "you can stop thinking about it. Do you want me to say the words?"

He looked at her.

"What happened to the team," she said, "is not your fault."

"How do you know that?" Ethan responded, looking away.

"You made a decision in the field. The NOC list was in the open, and you went after it."

He turned back to her, started to speak, but she cut him off.

"We both want the same thing right now," she said. "Now, we can go our own ways in order to do it, but that would be a mistake, wouldn't it?"

He nodded.

"All right then," she said.

"We need help," Ethan replied, "experienced people. But we don't have time. They have to be local."

"What kind of help?"

"IMF caliber."

"How are we going to do that?"

He reached into the electronics box she had packed and pulled out a black case about the size of a child's shoe box. Ethan plugged a cord into the box and stuffed the other jack into the wall. Then he connected the box to the laptop.

"I don't see where the KY Fifty-seven is going—"

He held up a hand. He flicked a small switch on the black box, and a green LCD lit up on the side of the box. Ethan typed a code into the laptop, which in turn appeared as an encrypted number on the box's LCD. It dialed a phone number. Moments later, the laptop's screen flashed a message:

IMF PERSONNEL DATABASE
ENTER PASSWORD NOW

Ethan typed in a password and the screen asked him:

CATEGORY?

He typed a single word:

DISAVOWED

Claire looked at him sharply; he looked right back at her.

Part Two

THE
DISAVOWED

Ground Zero

ETHAN AND CLAIRE CONTACTED THE POTENTIAL HELP they wanted in Prague, and arranged to meet them in Brussels, where they boarded a high-speed Eurotrain bound for London. This train was chosen because it was nonstop transit, and at speeds of 120 mph, it was unlikely that unwanted passengers would be boarding en route.

Sitting in a private business compartment across from two disavowed, disgraced former IMF agents seemed to Ethan an unusual way to ratchet up his mission. But then he'd worked in the intelligence field long enough to know that the lines between patriots and traitors, heroes and cowards, were constantly being redrawn by changing international boundaries and evolving political realities. Yesterday's enemy might be today's ally; that's the way it worked in espionage.

For agents to be disavowed from IMF, they had to have been caught or captured during a mission, screwed up in some significant, unforgivable way, or sold their services to more than one buyer at a time. When Phelps assembled and expanded his IMF teams he never looked for gung-ho flag wavers; he wanted realists, men and women who understood the complexities of modern governments and were comfortable with the invisible sociopolitical webs that bind industrialized nations. Countries had their public policies and their shadow policies, and it was in the shadow world that IMF teams operated. Of course, even in the shadow world, perhaps especially in the shadow world, IMF agents operated under a code of ethics: Never accept funds outside the system, never kill a nonsanctioned individual (unless that individual tries to kill you first), always reveal to headquarters any conflict of interest a mission might present. It was a short, clear list. And Ethan knew, looking at the two men sitting opposite, that these gentlemen had crossed a line somewhere. Probably several. They might have acquired information during the course of a mission that turned up for sale on the black market, or perhaps one of them used the framework of a mission to settle a private score. Something had happened. And whatever it was had been sufficient for Jim Phelps to release a highly trained, acutely skilled agent to the netherworld of the disavowed.

There was a time when Ethan would have nothing to do with such people, other than to neutralize their illegal actions. Ethan believed in ethics, even in a dirty business. But now that he had found himself on the disavowed list, and knew that he had landed there unjustly, he looked at these men differently than he would have one week ago. He was one of them. Who was to judge? Besides, he needed them. And necessity was always the most valued currency of the shadow world.

Accepting the one hundred fifty thousand dollars from Max had been a calculated gamble; if he could not flush Job and prove his own innocence, that money would seal his fate as a traitor to the IMF, the CIA, and the United States of America. He would be known as an employee of Max, and most certainly would be targeted by Kittridge for elimination. He would then be worse than disavowed; he would be labeled an accomplice in the murders of Phelps, Sarah, Jack, and Hannah. And in the espionage world of deep coverts, apprehension and trial were out of the question. A bullet in the back of the head while he sat in a Moroccan hotel bar would be the more likely proceeding. And Claire? By allying herself with Ethan, they both knew her fate was sealed with his.

None of which meant anything to the two disavowed IMF agents who sat looking at Ethan and Claire. These men were here for two reasons: money and Ethan Hunt. Both knew that if Ethan Hunt was in trouble—and he wouldn't have called them under any other circumstances—then there was money to be made. Second, if Ethan Hunt was leading the mission, whatever it turned out to be, it stood a reasonable chance of success. At least, they thought so until hearing what Ethan actually had in mind for them.

"It's a simple game," Ethan explained to them. He pointed to Franz Kreiger. "Ex-fil opens the pocket."

Then he pointed to Luther Stickell. "Cyber op lifts the wallet."

Right, simple, both men thought, everything is simple until you hear whose pocket and what's in the wallet.

Luther was an American from Chicago, though he now lived in the Alsace region of France. A muscular, soft-spoken black man in his mid-thirties, Luther always had a slightly bemused expression on his face, like he was picking up information from frequencies other people weren't privy to. Which was not a ridiculous assumption, since he was the best cyber ops agent Ethan had ever met. Luther had long ago passed from legendary status into being a godlike icon among the world's tech ops. The fact that Luther was disavowed IMF didn't matter to other wireheads. Luther was a genius, the Mozart of hackers, brilliant and unruly. When he was in sixth grade, for his school science project, Luther built a computer from scratch using parts pilfered from various appliances, vehicles, stores, and repair trucks. While other kids impressed teachers with clay models of Saturn, Luther was hacking into a local bank and temporarily increasing his father's bank account by fifty thousand dollars. When college came along Luther went legit, redoing the school's entire data processing systems in exchange for tuition. Naturally, even during his legit days he couldn't help the occasional prank, such as reprogramming a local television station's playback computer to broadcast eight solid hours of Alpo commercials, simply because his dog loved to watch them. After several brilliant years with the IMF, Luther went too far with one of his personal projects.

CIA electronics moles discovered that Luther was working on a plan to override launch codes for American nuclear weapons. Truthfully, he had no intention of sharing, using, or implementing his research in any way. Luther was just one of those people who wanted to know he could do it—no one else even had to know about it for Luther to gain satisfaction. It was all internal. Eugene Kittridge at one point had serious staff discussions about whether or not he should go beyond simply disavowing Luther Stickell; he wondered if Luther was too dangerous to live. But finally it was concluded within a soundless office somewhere in Langley that it might be even more dangerous for the CIA to kill Luther than to let him live; Kittridge was advised that Luther might have created some extraordinary viruses or digital worms to be activated in the event of Luther's untimely demise. And God alone knew if anyone living could neutralize a digital virus created by Luther Stickell. So it was decided to boot him out of the IMF and keep an eye on him. There was no doubt that if Kittridge, who at the moment was flying from London to Washington, knew that Luther Stickell was meeting with Ethan Hunt, any attempt at sleep would be futile.

Franz Kreiger, who sat next to Luther and across from Ethan and Claire, had the volatile, sneering countenance of a hormone-imbalanced teenager; just breathing seemed to piss the man off. There might be people worth liking in the world, but Kreiger hadn't met any of them; since he was French, he was inclined to believe that people he met outside of his country were probably not going to be up to his standards

117

anyway. All of which probably went into the reasons for his chosen profession: pilot. He could fly anything from an SST to a broomstick, with his particular area of expertise being helicopters. Kreiger once flew a chopper halfway across Siberia, evading radar, and plucked a prisoner out of a labor camp, dumped the chopper at a military airstrip, and stole a MIG, in which he outran half the Russian air force. That mission had become legendary in espionage circles, and though the Soviets claimed it never happened, the phantom mission cost two senior Russian generals their careers. Along with his aerial prowess, Kreiger was known to be an excellent entry man; he could break in or out of prisons, banks, palaces, you name it. Ethan guessed that Kreiger's disavowed status resulted from a ferrying mission of some kind, the cargo being stuff that strung-out people shoot into their veins. It didn't matter. Claire had worked with Kreiger on several occasions and vouched for his ability in the air and as a backup land operative for Ethan. He was a definite loner. But, then, so was Ethan. So, for that matter, was just about everybody associated with the IMF.

Kreiger tapped a finger on the table. "So tell me about this pocket I am to open. Bank job?"

"IMF mainframe," Ethan said, smiling.

Taking a moment to consider what Ethan had just said, Kreiger asked, "Where exactly is it?"

"In Langley."

Luther Stickell had been watching the green countryside out the window, half listening. Now he was listening.

"In Langley?" Luther said. "The one in Virginia, Langley?"

"Inside CIA headquarters at Langley," Kreiger added dismissively.

Ethan nodded. "That's right, ground zero."

Kreiger turned to Claire Phelps. "Is he serious?"

"Always," she said.

Mumbling to himself in French, Kreiger shrugged and looked at Ethan. "If we're going to Virginia, why don't we drop by Fort Knox? I can fly a helicopter right in through the lobby and set it down inside the vault, and it will be a hell of a lot easier than breaking into the goddamn CIA."

Luther Stickell stared at the light on the ceiling.

"What are we downloading?"

"Information," Ethan said.

"What kind?"

"Profitable."

"And payable on delivery," Claire added.

"Of course," Kreiger said, snorting. "Very profitable. And all those millions will do me good while I rot in an American jail."

"There is a certain amount of risk involved," Ethan said flatly.

"Do you really think so?" Kreiger said sarcastically, ripping off the top of a bottle of mineral water and guzzling it down. "Breaking into CIA headquarters. I don't see how there could be any risk attached to that."

"I don't know," Luther said, still staring at the light on the ceiling, thinking for his own amusement about the electrical wiring of the cutting-edge train, and how he could tap into it and probably override the sophisticated computer system that regulated their speed. "Langley. This I don't know."

Ethan leaned in toward him. "Now this doesn't sound like the Luther Stickell I've heard of. What did they used to call you? The Net Ranger? Phineas Phreak? The only man alive who actually hacked NATO GhostCom?"

Luther snapped his attention to Ethan's face. "There was never one piece of physical evidence that I had anything to do with that, that . . . that exceptional piece of work." His countenance was serious, but his eyes hinted at a smile within.

"You don't know what you're missing, Luther. This will be the Mount Everest of hack jobs. They write songs about people who do things like this."

But the smile vanished behind Luther's eyes as he looked at Ethan and Claire. "You're all kidding yourselves," he said soberly. "Even with top-of-the-line crypto. Cray access. STU Threes . . ."

"Kreiger can get all of that for you," Claire interrupted. She shot Kreiger a challenging look. "Right?"

"May take a little time," Kreiger said.

"May take a little time?" Ethan said, surprised. "That's not what Claire tells me about you."

And Luther was still mumbling about his high-tech shopping list, ". . . Thinking Machine laptops, I'm talking about the six-eighty-six prototypes—with the artificial intelligence Risc chip and military-grade fuzzy logic drivers . . ."

Ethan stared at Kreiger.

"Twenty-four hours," Kreiger said confidently.

Then Ethan looked back at Luther, who was thinking hard.

"And I get to keep all the equipment when we're done," Luther concluded.

"Luther," Ethan said, "I guess you're all out of excuses."

Luther snatched a bottle of mineral water from the ice bucket. He didn't open it, he just studied its construction. "I can't just hack my way inside, you know. Not at Langley. There's no modem access to the mainframe, it's in a stand-alone. No phone lines into that particular piece of silicon. I'd have to be physically sitting at the terminal, and I'm afraid I don't do entry work. Even if I did, you're talking about the CIA. There's no such thing as getting into that building, let alone walking into their computer room."

"Will you relax, Luther?" Ethan said. "It's worse than you think. The terminal's in black vault lockdown."

Luther looked like he was getting ill, and Kreiger simply looked disgusted. Of course, Kreiger always looked disgusted.

"They haven't missed a thing in that room," Ethan went on. "The mainframe requires significant cooling, meaning there is a large air duct. But the vents have laser nets over them. Inside, there are three intrusion countermeasure systems that can only be deactivated by authorized entry. Which, of course, we won't have."

He raised a finger. "The first system is sound-sensitive. Anything above a whisper sets it off."

Second finger. "The room's floor has pressure-sensitive panels. Even something light as a feather, a drop of water, paper clip, *anything*, and the alarm sounds."

Kreiger tossed his empty water bottle into the trash. Luther began rubbing his forehead, looking less intrigued by the second.

Then Ethan's third finger popped up. "And the final system detects any increase in temperature. The body heat of an unauthorized person in the room will trigger it. All three systems are state of the art. Very, very fine stuff."

Luther put his hands up in the air. "And you really think we can do this?"

Ethan gave them his most confident grin, and hoped that they bought it.

Claire sat in her compartment on the train late into the night, the train still barreling along. She looked at maps of Washington and Virginia, as well as a schematic of CIA headquarters. She took a deep drag off a Gauloise cigarette and blew the smoke out slowly. When Ethan tapped on her door and entered, she snuffed out the cigarette.

"Jim made me quit, and I couldn't get him to do the same thing," she said, pushing the ashtray away. "This is the first one I've had in a year."

Ethan nodded, looking awkwardly out at the blackness of the passing terrain. He handed her an envelope.

"It's cash," he said. "And a second passport. If anything goes wrong when we're inside, if you sense

122

even the slightest deviation, don't look over your shoulder, you walk away—hear me? Just walk away."

"You don't think we're going to make it."

"I didn't say that."

"In as many words."

He sat down next to her and said quietly, "Claire, I need you to be safe. I'm not sure I want you in on this at all, but if you go, you'll do it my way, and that means you walk if anything isn't right."

"What about you?"

"I lost the team. So now I need to know that you're safe."

"Ethan, like you said, someone knew we were coming to the embassy. And neither of us has to do what we're going to do in Langley. It's just that we want to."

She gave him a hug.

"You want a cigarette?" she said.

"I better not."

"I know. Me either. Something about riding on a train, though."

"Yeah. Well, get some sleep." He kissed her on both cheeks, then hugged her good night. But as he began to pull away she held on, their lips brushing as he turned his head. It was what he wanted, had wanted for some time, but he couldn't let it happen. They looked at each other, and then they kissed. Just for a moment.

And then he left.

Virginia

WITH THE EXCEPTION OF SURROUNDING ELECTRIFIED fences, sophisticated surveillance equipment at all entry points, movement detection devices, and dozens of patrolling uniformed guards carrying Heckler & Koch MP5 machine guns, CIA headquarters, carved out of the dense Virginia forest, resembled the campus of a small college. And the vast majority of CIA employees looked like office workers anywhere, except these workers, depending upon which section they worked in, were required to pass through at least four checkpoints before reaching their desks.

Tired and pale from the overnight trip from Prague to London to Washington, Eugene Kittridge was in no mood for small talk with security personnel and other colleagues as he passed through the checkpoints and walked briskly down the corridors toward a classified communications room. He'd spent the night rereading briefing dossiers on Ethan Hunt, Max, and a selection of disavowed IMF and CIA agents. His brain throbbed with names and the minutiae of personal histories. Each word in those dossiers was important, because it might be the smallest fact that offered a clue as to what an agent might be thinking or doing. Hunt's dossier was particularly exhausting to read because the guy was so accomplished and had run so many missions in different parts of the world; the possibilities with him were endless. He was an effective and dangerous operative, made even more so by the fact that he was now disavowed.

When Kittridge arrived in the communications room, Harry Barnes was already there, along with several other senior intelligence agents. A dozen multipurpose monitors formed a visual information bank, also known as a digiwall, near the conference table. Ten of the monitors were flashing photos of Ethan Hunt from various phases of his life, depicting him in a variety of disguises. Unfortunately for Kittridge, Barnes, and the rest of them, Hunt's disguises were remarkable.

"Those are good," Barnes said aloud, as the photos flashed through the monitors. "He could have been sitting across from us on the plane last night."

Kittridge's task force had spent the night and early morning hacking away at a variety of scenarios that might flush Ethan Hunt into the open. All of the ideas were, of course, top secret, especially since some of them, if implemented, were so far over the line of what the U.S. Constitution and Bill of Rights allowed that any attribution as to their origin might bring not only notoriety to their creator, but a prison sentence as well. Nothing would be put on paper, ever. Not when dealing with a disavowed IMF agent. The last thing Eugene Kittridge wanted in his life just about now was to have to sit in front of a Senate subcommittee, attempting to explain why taxpayers' money was spent to hire six hookers in Venezuela because two of them looked like Ethan Hunt's beloved ex-girlfriend. Nor did Kittridge want to have to explain how or why Hunt had been able to access the IMF disavowed list hours after being placed on it himself. Congress could get nasty in these matters. Particularly when it was Kittridge's mandate to root out the cracks and leaks in the CIA's shaky reputation. With the Aldrich Ames scandal still fresh in everyone's minds, whispers about a compromised disavowed file were not something an ambitious bureaucrat like Kittridge wanted himself associated with. If any heat was going to come down, Kittridge would think of a way to deflect it toward Harry Barnes.

But Harry Barnes was not without his own skills in office politics, and rather than have Kittridge transfer his sullen dissatisfaction with what happened in Prague onto Barnes's shoulders, Barnes waited for Kittridge to reach for his coffee, then pretended to continue a conversation that ostensibly he'd been leading prior to Kittridge's arrival.

"What I want to know," Barnes said, looking at agents Lowden and Marek at the end of the table, "is how Hunt accessed the disavowed file, even *after* we cut off his authorization code?"

Kittridge leaned back in his chair, balancing it on two legs.

"He may have used Phelps's code," Lowden suggested. "They were friends, and Phelps's was still valid for twenty-four hours."

"If that's the case," Barnes said, "we need to change IMF procedures and implement a system to immediately deactivate an agent's code upon—"

Kittridge slammed forward in his chair, the metal legs landing on the hard tile floor with a bang. "I can't believe what I'm listening to. Hunt just kicked us in the ass, and you guys are standing here trying to figure out what kind of shoes he had on!" He stood and stared at the tableful of agents. "I don't care how he accessed the disavowed file, I want to know why he did it. Is he recruiting? For what specific purpose?"

"Survival," Agent Marek said.

From somewhere in the building an alarm began to sound, a blaring, rhythmic alert.

Kittridge ignored it.

"Too shortsighted," he said. "He could survive by doing a Houdini. This guy's proactive, he initiates. That's why he accessed the disavowed file. Hunt has a plan and he's following it. The question becomes what does he want now, and where does he need to get it, and Barnes, what the *hell* is that noise?!"

An internal security agent entered the room. "Fire alarm, Gene."

"Oh, for . . . we don't have to evacuate, do we? Tell me that we don't. Not this morning."

"Sorry, it's S.O.P.," Barnes said to his boss, with a certain degree of pleasure.

"S.O.P.," Kittridge repeated flatly.

Two more internal security agents appeared in the room.

"Gentlemen, ladies," one of them said, "this is not

a drill, and we do have to follow procedure. So if you don't mind . . ." He pointed to the hallway.

"For God's sake," Kittridge muttered, walking out of the room.

They worked their way out to the beautifully trimmed lawns surrounding the main building and joined the crowds squinting in the bright noontime light. Kittridge looked for flame, smoke, or anything that could be credited as being the first actual fire at CIA headquarters in over twelve years.

Sirens from three approaching fire trucks shattered the quiet of the Virginia spring morning.

At exactly 9:23 A.M. the digital monitor behind the security station in the lobby of the CIA's main building lighted up like a Christmas tree. CIA security guard Richard MacIntyre stared at it with great interest. A veteran of Desert Storm and Bosnia, MacIntyre had participated in live-fire combat on six occasions, and was awarded a Purple Heart for rescuing three civilians from a sniper's fire in Bosnia while suffering two wounds to his left leg. Leaving the military and joining the CIA felt like a breather to him, and flashing lights on a computer monitor were not something that would rattle Mr. MacIntyre.

But since these lights indicated fire in several sections of the main building, he knew that decisions were going to have to be made, and made quickly. Fortunately, there were procedures in place for all of this. CIA firemen went only to areas where warning lights indicated, and they would be escorted by CIA security personnel.

The control panel provided a steady display of multiple security functions within the building: status locked or unlocked, in use or not in use, secure or not secure, activated fail-safe or not activated fail-safe, normal entry or restricted entry, and a half dozen other specific indications, fire among them. Of course, the fire sensors and alarms were hard-wired to a nearby CIA station, and the sophistication of the sensors could pinpoint down to a closet exactly where the trouble might be. The fire safety system was one of those hundred-million-dollar installations that no one ever expected to use, since fire in the CIA HQ was about as common as cigarettes in the surgeon general's office. Still, Mr. MacIntyre did not take this alarm lightly, since the possibility of a system malfunction was remote. The affected areas had bright red triangles pulsing above their sector numbers, and other readouts fed details pertaining to how many workers were in those sectors, names, and where they were scheduled to go in the event of just such an alarm.

At the desk with MacIntyre was another guard named Akers who, unlike MacIntyre, was not former military and had never seen combat or heavy action of any kind. Since this was reputedly the most secure building on the planet, Akers was somewhat taken aback to see the monitoring station flashing and buzzing. He looked to the senior guard for reassurance.

"Son, our prime directive is pretty much to stay at this desk until we're dead," MacIntyre said dryly.

For a moment, Akers thought he was serious. "Sir?"

Then MacIntyre pointed to the glass doors out

front, through which they could see three large yellow fire trucks rolling up. "Actually," MacIntyre said, "it's their problem."

A group of heavily equipped people rushed through the doors, flashing photo-security badges.

What amazed Akers was that most of the other CIA workers acted like they couldn't care less about the alarms. Workers from the designated sectors had evacuated, while workers not required to evacuate went about their business as on any other day.

But the firemen weren't taking it lightly. The first firefighter to the security desk was a fit young man wearing a safety helmet and black-framed glasses. "We picked up alarms in sectors three, seven, and twelve," he said to MacIntyre.

MacIntyre checked his screen.

"That's correct."

Three more firemen ran into the lobby, and seemed momentarily surprised to see a firefighter already at the security station. But he seemed in command.

"What sector's the air-conditioning?" the leader demanded.

"Twenty-one," MacIntyre answered, "but there's no alarm in sector twenty-one."

"I'm going in there and shutting it down just the same," the fireman replied.

"That's a negative, sir," MacIntyre said calmly. "No one enters any sector where the alarm isn't triggered."

"Do you *want* to blow the fire through the whole building?" said Ethan from behind the safety helmet's visor.

"Sir, nobody goes into any sector where the alarm did not go off," he repeated. "That's policy and you know it."

Listening to this exchange from his vantage point in the belly of the third fire truck was Luther Stickell, surrounded by computers, a mini–dish antenna, digital phones, scanners so sophisticated that the guys inside the tech labs of the CIA wouldn't believe an outsider had access to them. Of course, if they knew it was Luther Stickell out in the specially equipped truck, they'd believe anything.

Luther checked a schematic and ran a computation through one of his systems, then punched an enter key. Nothing changed. MacIntyre's screen hadn't changed. Luther dropped the schematic and tried his own version of the override that the schematic was supposed to have supplied.

Back at the desk, MacIntyre said to the fireman, "You can deploy your crew to the designated sectors, but we will not break policy for any other—"

"Check it again," the fireman said.

MacIntyre glanced at the screen. Sector 21 was now blinking.

"Okay," Akers said, also seeing the grid flash, "let's go."

He escorted the first team of firefighters down the hall, the team consisting of two men and a woman. Behind them, other firemen were following other CIA guards to various sectors supposedly on fire.

The third member of the team following Akers fell back and slipped into a ladies' room. She worked out of her fire gear to reveal a business suit underneath, complete with CIA ID badge and entry card. Claire Phelps took a last look at a computer printout of a man's ID photo, then dropped the printout into one of the agency's ubiquitous shredders, and set off for the cafeteria where this man, at this hour, was scheduled to be taking his coffee break.

William Donloe, the subject of Claire's interest, sat in the antiseptic atmosphere of CIA mainframe room 111. He tapped in updated data into the system and watched the screen accept his complicated set of codes and entry patterns. His wristwatch beeped, signaling a break. Following the same procedure he performed three or four times a day, he carefully logged out of the system, left the room, and activated the security system that would protect the integrity of this inner sanctum.

Donloe had worked at this job now for two years, a record. Most CIA data experts—and for this position workers had to pass total background checks—lasted only about six months in room 111. The isolation got to them. Only one worker at a time was allowed in this room. While at the computer, Donloe was not allowed to make or receive personal telephone calls; in fact, the phone in the room was wired to only one other handset, and that second phone was in a monitoring station, used only to report technical problems. Personal objects, like family photos, good luck charms, or decorations, were not allowed inside the computer room. There were no windows; the light level in the room never changed, nor did the temperature. It was a high-tech isolation tank, and after several months of working there, most people started to go nuts. They'd start talking to themselves, become withdrawn, moody; the security supervisor knew all the signs to look for and rotated the entry operators' duties to avoid the problem.

Donloe, however, was quickly becoming a legend within the ranks of CIA data operators. He thrived in room 111. He loved the isolation, the control, the predictability. The job made him feel important.

He heard somebody enter the lunch room, but didn't look up until the person sat down at the same table where he sat. It was Claire Phelps. Donloe had never seen this woman before—if he had, he certainly would have remembered her gorgeous face—but he glanced at her CIA identification badge, then back at his paper. What would be the point of engaging her in conversation? Women who looked like this were not a part of his universe. Claire threw him a polite smile and reached for one of the sections of the newspaper on the table; as she did, her hand passed over Donloe's cup of coffee, and from the pen in her hand, she deftly squirted a shot of a clear, tasteless, odorless liquid into the coffee. Then she picked up the paper's business section and retreated. As she withdrew from the table, she purposefully grazed Donloe's shoulder, then smiled apologetically. By the time Claire was back at her own cup of coffee, she had successfully tainted Donloe's cup and stuck a tiny gray-colored adhesive chip to his back.

The instant the chip took hold, a beep sounded back in Luther's fire truck. He looked at one of his monitors that broadcast an overlay of the CIA HQ floorplan. And there, right in the area designated as the data operators' lunch room, was a blue pulse. William Donloe was broadcasting a clear signal.

"Hi there," Luther said, pleased to see the homing device come to life.

In the lunch room Claire checked her watch, took a final sip of coffee, and headed for the door. William Donloe allowed himself to watch her walk out of the room, and even allowed himself a quick, vivid fantasy involving this stunning girl. Then she was gone and he returned to his newspaper.

Given the way the rest of Donloe's day was going to unfold, he might later, in a fit of religious guilt, believe what happened that day was divine retribution for his brief but wicked fantasy involving the woman he saw in the lunch room.

CIA security guard Akers delivered the two lead firemen to a service door in section 21.

"Air-conditioning's right through here!" he said, using a plastic coded card to open the door. As the firemen barreled inside, Akers looked confused, then irritated.

"Where's your third man?" he said, reaching for his walkie-talkie.

By then Kreiger had pulled a stun gun from his fireman's suit and jabbed into the guard's neck, immobilizing him. Dragging him inside, he pulled his black Teflon-coated combat knife and prepared to finish Akers on the spot, when Ethan whirled around, snapping a spin kick that knocked the knife out of Kreiger's hand.

Ethan grabbed Kreiger by the shoulders and hissed, "Zero body count."

"We'll see," Kreiger said, staring right back at Ethan, knowing they were too deep into the mission for chain-of-command debates.

"Tie him up and let's go," Ethan ordered.

The men stepped out of their fire suits, hid them, then buckled on equipment packs.

The service grille accessing the main duct was fixed to the ceiling with ten screws. Ethan went to work with a sound-baffled electric screwdriver. Before pulling out each screw, he sprayed an electronic coating into the socket, which fooled sensors into believing the grille was still in place. Ethan and Kreiger stashed their fire gear and slipped on arm- and leg-mounted magnetic suction cups, then started the long climb up the duct.

Luther monitored their movements in the duct by checking Ethan's Visco transmission and tracking the signals from their homing devices, which blinked over a blueprint grid of the building. Ethan reached a bed in the duct where it branched off in three different directions.

"Turn right," Luther told him from his command post in the truck, "and go straight up."

Moving vertically was slow and difficult, as each man had to plant the magnetic cups, then pull his body weight and the packs of equipment. The air-conditioning system was on automatic shutdown because of the fire alarms, so the air-intake ducts were getting warmer by the second.

Sweat from Ethan's face dripped down on Kreiger, who mumbled a curse in French.

"Silence from here on," Ethan said in his headset microphone, dragging himself up a difficult stretch of vertical duct.

"Yeah," Kreiger said, just to irritate Ethan.

Ethan looked down at him but kept moving, his muscles straining under the weight of the equipment.

"Button man is moving," Luther said, noting William Donloe's suddenly moving blue blip.

Donloe carefully folded his newspaper, took his Styrofoam cup of coffee, and headed into a hallway.

Somewhere inside the walls that Donloe walked past, Ethan and Kreiger crawled through a long horizontal stretch of duct, then up another shaft that was twelve feet of hot, hard climb. At the top, the duct turned horizontal again. Thirty feet ahead, Ethan saw light in the shaft. He crawled quietly forward until he could peer down through the grille where the light was coming from. Room 111, ground zero.

An inch below the surface of the vent's rectangular grille was a net of red laser beams, thick as a pencil. It was a simple system: if any of the beams were broken—by a fly, feather, or heavy puff of smoke—alarms triggered.

Turning to Kreiger, Ethan formed his hands into a triangle, prompting Kreiger to wriggle forward and hand Ethan a specially designed prism. He delicately lowered it into the laser net, allowing the prism to intercept beams without breaking them. A second prism was lowered on the other side of the vent and drew the intercepted beams up farther. He fixed the prisms with an adhesive to the edges of the vent, trapping the beams.

The opening was now clear.

He turned again and extended a hand. Kreiger slapped a small electronic screwdriver into Ethan's palm. Ethan lowered a magnetic strip next to each screw to catch it as it was released from its mooring. The screws holding this vent to its frame were not as long as those in sector 21, so the process went quickly. One at a time he lifted the screws and snatched them off the strip with his teeth. When he had all six screws, he spit them into one hand, while holding the grille with the other. Carefully stuffing the screws into a pocket, he lowered the grille, turned it sideways, and raised it up through the opening, handing it off to Kreiger.

"Cold tube," he mouthed, and was handed a length of flexible plastic pipette connected to a thermos-sized canister in Kreiger's hip pack. Ethan fed the tubing down the open vent and aimed it toward the thermostat atop the mainframe. The security temperature sensor was rigged to signal a rise in the room temperature; however, lowering the room temperature did not arm the system. Once the tube was in place opposite the sensor, Ethan signaled Kreiger, and he began blowing cold air into the room, enough to counterbalance Ethan's body heat.

Ethan cinched up the pivots on a gymnast's safety harness belted around his waist and hips, and Kreiger hooked high-test nylon lines to the cleats on Ethan's harness. Edging toward the opening, Ethan angled his body headfirst and began descending into the room.

Kreiger was wedged inside the metal air duct, holding the lines that kept Ethan suspended in midair, gently lowering him via the sound-dampened pulleys. Headfirst, Ethan's upside-down view of the computer was surreal. The walls were intensely white, as were the pressure-sensitive tiles on the floor. Colored lights embedded in the Cray blinked on and off. There was an unearthly silence in the room, and Ethan could hear the blood pumping in his heart and the air leaving his mouth. He had never been in a place that was so quiet, and so strange. Dangling over a dozen alarm systems, he knew that if he made one mistake, he would become Kittridge's perfect prize— a mole caught while suspended in the air right smack dab in the center of CIA headquarters. How convenient. If that happened, there would be no explaining that he was actually trying to prove his innocence. Kittridge's prosecution would be a slam-dunk case. Caught in the act trying to steal national security secrets, all to try to catch the real mole? Yeah, that excuse would fly about as far as a Thanksgiving turkey. Not only that, but at this moment Ethan was at the total mercy of Kreiger, who held the pulley lines. One error by Kreiger—a man Ethan had never worked with and whom he already knew he didn't like—and the mission would terminate in disaster. And what of Claire? What if she didn't get to Donloe? What if she did, but Donloe didn't drink his coffee? The blood rushed to Ethan's head and he felt his neck swelling and eyes bulging as he reached the level of the heat sensor. Slowly moving past it, he carefully positioned the plastic tubing so that it would affect the sensor gradually. He realized he hadn't taken a breath in quite a while; he could not risk inhaling loudly, so he silently sucked tiny gasps of cool air from the sterile atmosphere in the room.

Down in the hallways, William Donloe traveled briskly back to his computer room.

He passed through two internal checkpoints, then reached the outer entrance to 111. There, even though the security supervisor knew Donloe by face, she still required him to present his ID badge and entry card. Then, to gain final access, he rested his chin on a curved mount and stared into a retinal scanner.

As the computer room door opened to admit Donloe, Ethan was jerked upward, suspended just below the vent. No time to disappear.

William Donloe entered his domain.

As he walked to the work station, Donloe paused and hunched over, holding his stomach with his free hand. Twelve feet above, suspended horizontally in the air, was Ethan Hunt, the only thing separating him from William Donloe and a thirty-year prison sentence being a nylon harness and a pulley system controlled by Kreiger.

He dangled like a giant Christmas ornament, holding his breath, each second seeming like hours.

What the hell happened to the T-19 compound Claire was supposed to put in the man's coffee? Ethan wondered, praying that Donloe would remain hunched over.

Donloe set his coffee cup on the rubberized work station counter, pulled out the keyboard, and checked the documents he was preparing to translate and encode into the system. He felt queasy but prided himself on not being subject to the usual colds, viruses, and flus that were passed around among the employees in the building.

Above him, Ethan Hunt turned slowly, holding his breath, questioning his own sanity at even attempting this heist.

In the truck Luther Stickell leaned back and stared helplessly at the Visco transmission.

Kreiger held on to the ropes, his muscles screaming from being in one position for so long.

Donloe took a deep breath, reached for his coffee, and took a sip. He cleared his throat, and the sound bounced around the room like an explosion.

Ethan's body was rigid, motionless, but he knew he couldn't keep it that way for long, and he could feel the strain in the nylon rope as Kreiger held on from above.

Donloe started typing, stopping only to wipe sweat from his face.

Just when Ethan felt he couldn't hold his position for another second, Donloe abruptly stopped typing, slowly leaned back in his chair, and began to look up. It was as if he had suddenly sensed Ethan's presence in the room.

But as Donloe's head tilted back, he reached for the wastebasket hooked to one side of the work station and jerked it in front of his face in just enough time to catch the vomit that shot violently from his mouth.

He stood, vomited again into the wastebasket, then rushed to the door, hitting a yellow button that opened it. The door shut behind him.

But even in Donloe's state of overwhelming nausea, he remembered to stuff his key card into the exterior security slot. Back inside the mainframe room the pressure-sensitive floor tiles lit up, and a digital screen by the door flashed: INTRUSION COUNTERMEASURES——ON.

Kreiger moved himself back in the shaft to gain more leverage, then began lowering Ethan steadily toward the floor. He stopped when Ethan was opposite the work station. Unfortunately, the keyboard remained three feet out of Ethan's reach. Ethan looked up at the nylon lines. They were positioned at such an angle in the duct that if he could move them a foot or so to the side, he could reach the keyboard. He felt Kreiger straining under the body weight, and worried that he was running out of time.

So Ethan swung himself back and forth in ever-increasing arcs, gaining momentum. Blood rushed back and forth in his head and perspiration coated the exposed areas of his face with a faint sheen. Gathering all of his strength he performed a controlled acrobatic flip, forcing the ropes to move far enough to put him within reach of the computer keyboard.

Above, Kreiger steadied himself in the duct, sweating and biting his lower lip to keep from groaning out loud.

Luther Stickell watched intently, fighting back his own case of motion sickness from watching Ethan swinging in the harness.

When Ethan stabilized his position, he realized he was still just out of reach from the keyboard. So he gathered his strength and performed a midair sit-up that brought him around and placed him in front of the work station, looking like a skydiver suspended in free fall. Stomach muscles burning, he nodded rapidly, which was Luther's cue to speak, and quickly.

"Okay, here we go," Luther said, eyes riveted to the

Visco monitor. "Type this password: AW-nine-six-B-six. Then return."

Ethan followed the instructions, perspiration gathering on his forehead.

"Now go to the files menu," Luther continued. "Find the NOC list file." He watched and waited, and when the file came on-screen, he whispered, "There. Type 'open NOC list.'"

Ethan did so, his stomach muscles screaming for relief. Sweat rolled down his face, along his neck, and soaked into his collar.

"Put your disk in the slot to the right. Double click on the NOC list."

In his right breast pocket was a blank 3.5-inch diskette, specially formatted by Luther to the Cray's unique specifications. He slid it into the "write only" slot on the machine, and listened to the soft whirring sound that meant the diskette had been accepted. As quiet as the sound was, in the silence of the computer room it roared in Ethan's brain like an avalanche.

He tensed and waited for an alarm.

None came.

So he performed the double-click on the selected file, and from inside the computer came more muffled, whirring sounds, indicating that the Cray computer was performing a function.

"Okay, good," Luther said. "It's scrolling. Okay, now we're going to download. Edit menu. Select 'copy to disk.'"

Ethan did it, but the muscles of his lower back were beginning to spasm from being in this awkward position.

Luther saw the strain on Ethan's face.

"You're knocking on the door," Luther said. "Don't leave."

A "downloading" prompt appeared on the screen, and Luther's excitement quivered in Ethan's Visco earpiece. "You're downloading," he said, in a voice that indicated history was being made. "When it's all green up there, it's done."

The NOC list began quickly scrolling across the screen, and was visible to Luther on the monitor. Real names and locations were being matched to code names and cover operations. The deepest secrets of U.S. intelligence operations would be in complete jeopardy if the list left this room.

"Holy mother of God," Luther whispered.

In the air duct, Franz Kreiger heard Luther's elation, but felt none of it. He and Ethan were still stuck in the bowels of CIA headquarters, and a long way from anywhere that could be called safe. Keeping Ethan steady was ripping Kreiger's muscles to shreds. It felt like someone was running a blowtorch up and down his arms and legs. The sweat fell off of him in rivulets.

Then he heard a sound that didn't come from the earpiece or the computer room.

A faint scratching sound coming from the sheet metal duct, just a few feet away from Kreiger's head.

He looked up to see a rat shuffle into view. A fat, bold rat stared at Kreiger.

Kreiger stared back.

Puzzled by Kreiger's lack of response, the rat inched forward. Kreiger spit at it. Missed. It moved forward. And it wasn't that Kreiger was afraid of the rodent. He was allergic to rat fur. His eyes began to water, his nose twitched. Kreiger felt himself about to sneeze.

Luther's voice came over the system again.

"You've done it. Eject the disk."

Whatever strength remained in Ethan's body was necessary for him to reach forward, pop the disk, and slide it back into the Velcro pocket of his body suit.

Then he just let himself dangle a moment, relaxing his muscles and catching his breath.

He felt the ropes shift.

In the shaft Kreiger dragged the two pulley lines together in order to free up one of his hands. Then, as the rat reached his face, Kreiger went for his knife.

And in the moment he reached to kill the rat, he lost his leverage and the ropes slipped.

Ethan dropped like a brick toward the pressure-sensitive floor.

At the last possible moment Kreiger snatched the lines and tugged, leaving Ethan spread-eagle, body locked, one inch above the tiles.

Ethan snapped his head sideways to keep his nose from hitting the floor. He gasped and struggled to hold his body position, as Kreiger fought to reposition himself and regain leverage.

Finally, Kreiger began to crank him up.

A line of sweat trickled down Ethan's forehead, fell to the tip of his nose, and formed a large drop. He turned his head, and in the same instant the bead of sweat dropped toward the pressure-sensitive tiles. That would be enough to set off alarms that would seal the building and bring hundreds of security personnel into action.

Ethan's left hand swooped down in an instinctive motion, and snatched the drop of sweat in midair, trapping it in his latex glove.

William Donloe tried to leave the men's bathroom three times, but each time he was overtaken by another overwhelming wave of nausea, and rushed back to the stall. Given the volume of fluid expelled from his body in the last ten minutes, he could barely remain on his feet; his head felt as if it had been put in a centrifuge. Finally, there was simply nothing left inside to come out.

He splashed water on his face, trembling from the thought that he was being overtaken by a violent virus that might be killing him. And only God and a few scientists knew what kind of awful chemical weapon CIA might be developing in their labs. Could something have gotten loose? A trip to the building's infirmary was in order, but first he had to feel well enough to go there. Second, he had to close the files he'd been working on back in the computer room. So he gamely staggered out of the men's room and started once again to work his way through the various security checkpoints that led to his work station.

"Button man moving," Luther Stickell whispered into his microphone, watching a traveling blue dot.

At the moment, Ethan was being hoisted back up to the vent by Kreiger. Suddenly, Kreiger abruptly stopped cranking, leaving Ethan dangling five feet from safety.

Ethan frantically tapped the Visco glasses to warn Kreiger of Donloe's approach.

Kreiger gazed down through the opening at Ethan and shook his head.

Ethan glared, silently mouthing "What's wrong?!"

Kreiger took one hand away from the nylon rope and extended it downward, snapping his fingers open and shut.

Luther spoke again to Ethan, "Get out of there—get out of there—"

Gesturing toward the door, Ethan tapped his watch urgently.

But Kreiger kept snapping his hand open and closed. He wanted the diskette.

"Pull me up, you bastard," Ethan mouthed.

Kreiger just stared implacably and shook his head.

"Hey, he's at the vault," Luther urged. "He's coding in. One yellow, two yellows. Toast!"

There was no time to debate.

"You're not moving," Luther said, exasperated. "Toast!"

Ethan pulled out the diskette case and handed it to Kreiger, who then hauled Ethan up into the vent.

"Merci," Kreiger whispered, stowing the diskette inside his vest.

But as he reached to pull Ethan from the opening, Kreiger's right knee bumped the combat knife he'd used to kill the rat, and the knife slid into the opening and dropped.

Momentarily frozen, both Ethan and Kreiger watched the knife turn end over end, falling toward the floor.

The steel entry door clanked as Donloe passed the

retinal scan, releasing the locking mechanism. A split second before the door opened, the knife fell point-first into the work station, its tip embedding in the hard rubber surface of the desk area.

Ethan and Kreiger stared at the knife in total shock and disbelief.

Then Donloe stepped into the room, still bent over from his ordeal.

When he reached the work station and pulled the keyboard out on its movable tray, he noticed the knife sticking straight up and a few inches to his left. For him, it was like returning to his apartment and finding a spaceship parked in his living room. For several moments, he thought he was hallucinating.

But then he touched the knife. It was real. How could this be possible? A weird prank, perhaps? Donloe looked straight up at the air-intake vent. It was there, as usual, the red laser net crisscrossed in its activated pattern.

His heart raced as he sat down and booted up the screen. The prompt that appeared was even more disturbing to him than the knife:

Keystroke Log—File Download
11/18/95   9:58 am

No, not possible. He had been in the bathroom puking his guts out at the time of this log record, just six minutes ago. Could the Cray 3 have malfunctioned? One chance in a billion. Had he given it a command before he left? No, even in his weakened state, he would remember that. If someone else had entered the room in his absence, his security supervisor would have indicated so. This download was an impossibility.

But, then, so was the knife.

While Donloe sat and contemplated the unthinkable, Ethan and Kreiger crawled quietly away, placing smoke bombs as they went to make certain that the fire alarms would stay active.

Back in the computer room, Donloe finally resigned himself to the terrible, perplexing reality that confronted him. He picked up the emergency phone on the work station and pushed four buttons, knowing that life as he knew it was about to change.

Kittridge had waited out fifteen minutes of the fire alarm, then pulled rank and brought his team back to the conference room.

"Think," he yelled at Barnes and the assembled agents. "For Christ's sake. You guys are mired in details. Forget about Hunt's high school report card. Open your minds, it's got to be staring us in the face. Ethan Hunt has recruited two disavowed IMF agents. Why? He wants something. There is the question. What does Ethan Hunt *want?"*

"Same thing he wanted in Prague," Barnes said boldly. "Same thing he's always wanted. The NOC list."

"Okay, but the list simply isn't available to him. Where is the list vulnerable?"

Several of the agents smiled uneasily.

"Other than here, of course," Kittridge added, with a brief laugh. Nervous chuckles volleyed across the table.

Behind Kittridge, on the other side of the room, a

phone began to ring softly. There were half a dozen phones on that station, but the fact that this particular one was ringing caught everyone's attention. An agent answered the phone and listened intently, his face slowly losing color. Then he turned and looked at Kittridge, extending the phone, the bearer of exceedingly bad news.

"For you," he said, his voice a whisper.

Kittridge hesitated, several thoughts colliding in his head, dark possibilities that were improbable, but . . .

"Kittridge, yep," he said, grabbing the phone.

William Donloe spoke to him in a halting, confused voice. When he finally spat out what he was trying to say, Kittridge confirmed in his mind a possibility that had been creeping up on him all morning—that this was going to be the single worst day of his life.

The four of them—Ethan, Claire, Luther, and Kreiger—jammed into the front seat of the fire truck as Kreiger piloted the vehicle down a deserted country lane back toward the escape car. No one had said a word since they'd left CIA HQ.

Kreiger looked smug and confident, the diskette safely tucked away inside his vest. Claire was exhausted, leaning her head against Ethan's shoulder and closing her eyes. Ethan gazed at the passing scenery, his thoughts traveling off to some private place.

And Luther Stickell looked troubled.

The adrenaline high of hacking into technically the most secure building in the world, actually accessing a CIA stand-alone Cray 3, and walking out of there with the NOC list had lasted for about five minutes.

Then reality set in like a cold shower on a winter morning.

What the hell were they doing? The NOC list was as sensitive a repository of information as could be found in the free world. Literally, thousands of lives were at stake with that list in the open. Diplomatic relationships could be soured or destroyed. It was not out of the realm of possibility that, in the wrong hands, the NOC list could be used to kick-start cold wars between the U.S. and at least half a dozen other countries. Secrets embedded within this list could even be used to ignite a hot war. What the hell were they doing?

The only mitigating factor for Luther was that he trusted Ethan Hunt. But what was Ethan doing messed up with a guy like Kreiger, why was the IMF's golden boy operative suddenly on the disavowed list, and why was Ethan willing to risk his life to steal the NOC list? He couldn't possibly hope to get away with all this, could he? These were questions Luther had been quietly asking himself for a couple of days now. The answers didn't really matter all that much to Luther, given the way the CIA and the IMF had treated him in the past—he would probably have done this job just for the money and the chance to launch the greatest hack in the history of cyber ops. Still, the NOC list had disturbing implications. And though he trusted Ethan—even though Ethan had not shared his overall plan with him or Kreiger—it would be comforting to know that the list wasn't going to be used for a bloodbath. Luther knew he'd sleep better having that certainty tucked away in his cranium.

"I don't know," Luther said aloud. "I really don't know."

Ethan glanced over at him, knowing exactly what Luther was thinking.

"Let's just get back to London," Ethan said to Luther.

"It sure as hell ain't going to be safe here," Luther said.

"No, I wouldn't think so," Ethan replied, settling back, knowing that within hours Kittridge would place the four of them on a classified "most wanted" list. What Ethan counted on to buy time was the fact that Kittridge wouldn't want to broadcast to every law-enforcement agency in the world that CIA's NOC list had been stolen right out from under his nose. Ethan knew that Kittridge would want to try and recover the list himself, and that provided a window of opportunity. Certainly, Ethan had no intention of letting the NOC list out in the open. Like Luther, he fully understood the implications of the information they'd stolen. And he did not want innocent blood on his hands. But in a high-stakes game such as this, he needed a big bankroll to attract the right players. The NOC was as big a bankroll as anyone in the intelligence community could conceive of.

But it did bother Ethan that Luther seemed to be the only member of his current team troubled by what they'd done, and by what was in their possession. Kreiger, clearly, was in it for the money, and anything that stood in the way of that, including a CIA guard, was fair game. Claire had said nothing about the NOC list; she professed to care only about revenge for Jim's death. But at what cost? Ethan wondered. She was, however, following Ethan's plan, so it was difficult for him to question her lack of interest in the ultimate disposition of the list. And as they sped through the countryside, he took a hard look at himself. Yes, he wanted to flush Job from his cover, whoever Job was. But using the NOC list as bait was a risky, perhaps fatal, business. What if Ethan was killed before the disposition of the NOC list was determined? Then a lot of people would die because of Ethan's quest. That thought weighed heavily upon him. Especially when he glanced over at Kreiger, and recalled the knife Kreiger had pulled on the guard and then dropped into the computer room. It was a very specific knife, made out of a hybrid plastic, hard enough to cut metal yet able to pass through security detection devices. Even in his line of work, Ethan had not seen many custom blades like that. In fact, the last one he'd seen was protruding from the chest of Sarah Norman. It was a blade designed for killing human beings, and for no other purpose. Kreiger was quite comfortable with that blade, and had obviously used one in the past. Ethan had no choice but to work with disavowed agents right now, but he certainly wished he knew more about the reasons Kreiger was on that list.

The group in the CIA conference room had been reduced, for security purposes, to three people: Kittridge, Barnes, and William Donloe.

Having alerted Kittridge to the potential breach, Donloe then spent half an hour checking and rechecking his computer, confirming the alarming fact that the download had, indeed, been the NOC list. And for the last fifteen minutes Kittridge had sat beside Donloe, making him review every possible detail of his day since arriving at Langley that morning. Donloe's coffee was already undergoing an intense lab analysis.

CIA security guard Akers had already been debriefed, still confounded and embarrassed by the fact that he'd been hog-tied by two firemen inside CIA headquarters, but grateful for the younger of the two, who had, presumably, saved his life. Akers, of course, had no idea what the two firemen did once they disappeared into the duct. Only Barnes, Kittridge, and Donloe were aware of the full extent of this disaster.

And Kittridge, seasoned bureaucrat that he was, did his best to convince Donloe that this unthinkable breach of security was, somehow, completely Donloe's fault.

Finally, Kittridge rose from the conference table and signaled Barnes to join him on the far side of the room.

He whispered instructions.

"You and I know about this . . . and that's where it stops. Understand? It never happened."

"I understand," Barnes said.

"Do you also understand that it could only have been Ethan Hunt?"

"I'd say that's a pretty good guess, sir."

"It's not a guess, Barnes."

Barnes nodded discreetly toward Donloe.

"What about him?"

"Record?" Kittridge asked.

"Spotless."

Kittridge leaned toward Barnes's left ear.

"I want him manning a radar tower in Alaska by the end of the day. Just mail him his clothes."

Kittridge exited the room without turning to look at Donloe.

Donloe tracked him with his eyes until the door clicked shut, then looked expectantly at Harry Barnes, known to be a reasonable and fair man, one who would certainly know that this security breach was not Donloe's fault. Whoever did this had to penetrate security at the very core of the CIA HQ, which was not the responsibility of William Donloe. Surely, Barnes knew that.

Harry Barnes tried to think of a pleasant, acceptable way to inform Donloe of his new assignment.

But the longer the silence lay like a corpse in the room, the clearer it became to William Donloe that it was going to be a long, long time before he ever again touched his beloved Cray 3.

London

MOST OF THE LAST FIVE YEARS OF ETHAN HUNT'S LIFE had been spent traveling to nearly every country and major city in the world, and usually on short notice. There were several cities he hoped never to see again. There were also cities, London being chief among them, that he treasured. IMF travel didn't afford chunks of free time, but whenever he found himself anywhere near Great Britain, he'd steal a day or two to visit his favorite museums, get lost in the amiable atmosphere of the neighborhood pubs, or walk the streets and think about the centuries of life that had gone on here, shaping so much of Western civilization. Since history had always been his favorite subject in school, this cradle of culture had always proved nourishing to him.

This trip, of course, was different. Twenty-four

hours ago he was crawling through air-intake ducts in the heart of CIA HQ, and now he sat in a tawdry office building near Waterloo Station, using a safe house that had the cover of a travel agency. Just being in the city this time grated on his nerves and saddened the quieter places within his soul, because London reminded him of Sarah Norman and drew his thoughts back to that awful night in Prague.

He thought it ironic to be sitting in this stale-smelling old London flat, thumbing through a Bible. It was the same Bible he'd taken from the Prague safe house and used as a reference to contact Max. He turned to the Book of Job, popped open his Apple Powerbook, and typed in the appropriate chapter and verse to make its cyberspace journey to this mysterious arms dealer. If God only knew, Ethan thought, what his Word was being used for.

He logged into the biblical website and typed this message:

MAX—now might be an excellent time to interpret Scripture face to face. Meet on TGV, noon tomorrow. Take seat 27. Bring our mutual friend Job.

Ethan sent the message, and sat back.

Luther Stickell stood in the flat's kitchenette, working on a small modification of a cell phone.

Kreiger was in the next room, sipping a Guinness and watching CNN. Claire was curled up on a couch, trying to doze without much success.

"Contacting your buyer?" Kreiger asked, glancing at Ethan.

Ethan ignored him.

"Ethan?"

Silence.

"Ethan?" Kreiger said, raising his voice to a volume impossible to ignore. "Do I have to call you Mr. Hunt?"

Still Ethan stayed focused on the computer, checking to see if his message had been successfully sent on the Internet.

Kreiger walked over and saw the text of the message on-screen.

He slapped the Bible right out of Ethan's hand.

"You're not going to any meeting without me," he said.

"My contact is extremely shy," Ethan answered, watching his computer screen.

Luther and Claire carefully watched this confrontation. Nobody had gotten much sleep in the past two days. Things could get ugly fast.

Kreiger lifted the little blue diskette out of his vest and wagged it in the air, just in front of Ethan's face.

"I don't think you're in any position to give orders," Kreiger said, "do you? Not while I'm holding this."

Claire moved forward. She knew Ethan well enough to know that when his eyes began to darken, no matter how calm his face appeared, it was a bad sign.

"Kreiger," she said, her voice a warning.

He snapped her a glance. *"Lâchez-moi,"* he said testily.

Ethan flipped open a briefcase. "Don't you mean this, Kreiger?" he said, displaying a disk identical to the one Kreiger held. Ethan stuck it into the pocket of his jacket.

"That isn't it," Kreiger said, not totally convinced. "That's not the list."

"What's the matter?" Ethan said, suddenly grinning. "You don't know this trick?" He turned sideways and pulled the pocket wide open for inspection. Kreiger took a cursory glance: nothing. Ethan walked to the center of the room, where Luther and Claire looked on, mystified. "So where did it go?" Ethan asked, feigning consternation. "It's just . . . *gone!*"

He reached over to Claire, slipped a hand into a pocket of her denim trousers, and withdrew a blue diskette. "But not too far."

He laid the disk flat on his right palm. "I know what you're thinking, Kreiger. You're thinking . . . back in the computer room . . . I was up here . . . he was down there. Was he carrying two disks?"

He rotated his hand, turned it palm up again. The diskette was gone. He extended his left hand now. There it was, plain as day. "So hard to keep track of these things." He turned his hand over, turned it back up. Both hands were now exposed. And no diskette.

Kreiger's eyes narrowed; there was a visible reddening of his face beneath his splotchy beard. "Where is it?"

Ethan patted his pockets with exaggerated motions, panicked. "I thought you had it!"

Then he grinned.

"Do you actually think I'd let you have the NOC list?"

Claire laughed. Kreiger found none of it amusing

158

and threw her an icy look. When he turned back to Ethan, Ethan had two disks, one in each hand.

Kreiger sucked in a shot of air through his nose. "Try any sleight-of-hand with my money and I'll cut your throat," he said, jerking the diskette from his own pocket. On his way out the door, Kreiger tossed the diskette like a Frisbee toward a wastebasket. Bull's-eye. He slammed the door behind him.

Ethan bent down and picked up the Bible from the floor, and noticed that the inside cover was stamped DRAKE HOTEL, CHICAGO. PLACED BY THE GIDEONS.

He stared at the imprint for several seconds, as an involuntary chill shot through his system.

Chicago, he thought. Drake Hotel. That was Jim Phelps's last stop before Prague. In fact, Ethan and Jack had kidded him about it just a few days ago. And since Ethan knew Jim Phelps was not a religious man, Jim's bringing this Bible all the way to Prague with him was certainly for a specific use.

He closed the book and put it down. Claire was looking at him, and Ethan wondered if she could read what was going through his mind at the moment.

She had an apologetic look on her face.

"I'm sorry about him," she said.

Ethan stared at her, and waited for more.

Then she clarified what she meant. "Kreiger. He was my call, but I didn't expect this. I'm very sorry."

Ethan shrugged. "He did his job." He looked at the blacked-out window, then back at Claire. "We all did what we had to do."

"Well," she said, "I'm going to give sleep another chance."

She kissed Ethan on the cheek, then went off to one of the rooms to sleep, leaving Luther and Ethan alone. Ethan waited until Claire was gone, then walked to the wastebasket and retrieved Kreiger's blue diskette. He dropped one of the others into the basket in its place.

Luther chuckled. "Kreiger had the NOC list."

Ethan nodded soberly. "Now I want you to hold on to it."

The two men exchanged looks; it had been a long time since anyone had entrusted Luther with anything.

"What makes you trust me?"

"Because if you knew what you were getting into, you never would have done it."

Luther took the diskette from Ethan, and said firmly, "I'll tell you this, I'm not letting this list get out in the open."

"Exactly. That's your job." Ethan nodded toward the cellular rig that Luther was modifying. "What's the range of that thing, anyway?"

"It's hard to tell. I'm going to have to be close to Max."

"Okay, I'll get you close."

Claire appeared suddenly, poking her head into the room. "Ethan?"

They both looked at her.

"I need to talk to you," she said quietly.

He walked into the room. She pointed to the small television on the dresser.

There on CNN, a news anchor was reporting some kind of drug story. Ethan looked at Claire quizzically.

She pointed to the screen, looking grim, as the anchor continued:

". . . the unlikely setting, a farm in the heartland of America, the state of Wisconsin, where federal agents claim to have broken the brain trust behind an international drug ring. For a report we go live now to CNN correspondent Denton Jones in the state capital. Denton?"

The reporter was on the steps of a courthouse. "Authorities have identified the pair as Margaret Ethan Hunt and Donald Hunt."

Dumbfounded, Ethan turned up the volume.

". . . and here they are now . . ."

There, shackled with wrist and ankle chains, flanked by U.S. marshals and deputies, were Ethan's mother and his uncle Donald, being dragged past a pack of reporters and photographers, who shouted questions and snapped photos.

"They were apprehended in a dawn raid by DEA as a part of a major sting operation for the illegal manufacture of methcathinone, known on the street as 'cat.' "

Ethan was numb with disbelief.

". . . similar to methamphetamines, cat is seen by officials as one of the most powerful and dangerous drugs in the world. Some thirty-four cat labs have been seized, but the recently widowed Mrs. Hunt and her brother-in-law are believed involved in a global drug distribution network."

Ethan's mother and uncle were loaded into a waiting van that was trailed by two unmarked follow cars.

Then a public official appeared from the courthouse

and was swamped by reporters. He approached the bank of microphones, listened to several of the questions shouted his way, then answered. "I think it's sad, really," he said. "I mean, look at those people. Farmers, unless they're a conglomerate, are always operating on paper-thin margins. And I'm afraid what we have here is a case of a naive, desperate widow with a lot of financial problems, who chose to make money through illegal means. It's quite tragic, but our aim is to take these drugs off the street, and in order to do that we have to root out the supply chain, no matter where we find it."

The official finished his comment and departed, while the reporter quickly swung to the CNN camera. "That was John Fairchild, DEA special agent in charge of this investigation. Officials tell me that international law enforcement agents are expected to arrive here later today to question the Hunts. So, obviously, there is a lot more of this story waiting to unfold. And when it does, we'll be there. This is Denton Jones, CNN, live in Madison, Wisconsin."

Ethan snapped his hand at the button and shut the television off.

"Kittridge," he said, a quiet, sharp edge to his voice.

Claire shook her head. "Bastard!"

Ethan's demeanor was dark and icy; suddenly he had the cold-eyed calm of a professional killer.

She instinctively stepped back from him. "Well, what are you going to do?"

He pointed at the television. "Kittridge is expecting me to call," he said, striding toward the door. "I'm going to the station." Ethan crossed the living room, yanking open the front door. "And I'm going to call him."

There had been no doubt in Ethan's mind, from the moment he exploded his way out of the location green restaurant in Prague, right through the CIA break-in, that Kittridge was going to come after him, and hard. The stakes were high. They were not dealing with the plans for an experimental weapon, or advance information about NATO troop movements in the Middle East. This was the NOC list. This was everything. If that list got out into the open, the CIA might as well turn itself into a temporary morgue to house the bodies that would start stacking up. Bodies and careers, with Kittridge's being among the most prominent.

Ethan knew that Kittridge, after figuring out what happened at Langley, would go straight for the bottom of the deck, but he had miscalculated about what cards would be in that deck. For Kittridge to involve Ethan's mother and uncle, two innocent, unaware civilians, to drag them across global television as drug dealers, was a clear announcement that the game had escalated. It was all or nothing.

As a steady rain beat down on the pavement, Ethan emerged from a side street outside the safe house, and glanced up to the third floor, where he caught sight of Claire, who was watching him from the bedroom window. Claire had not said much since arriving in London, and at this moment she looked troubled, reflective, like she hadn't wanted him to leave. Or at least, to leave without her.

Without acknowledging her look, he cut over to Waterloo Station, and hurried past pedestrians down an escalator and straight to a bank of telephones. He pounded a number into the keypad.

Eugene Kittridge had not left CIA HQ since the security breach. The building contained several suites for agents tracking a hot assignment, and Kittridge had spent the night there. Orchestrating the arrest of Margaret and Donald Hunt had not been a simple matter. The attorney general of the United States, the directors of DEA and FBI, had to be consulted and involved. Those other agencies were not given the true reason for the frame-up, but Kittridge advanced the plan as a national security emergency involving a rogue IMF agent, and that was enough to grease the gears of government. For the moment, the theft of the NOC list remained inside Kittridge's tight circle, but he knew that his "need-to-know" classification on the matter could remain buttoned down only for another twenty-four hours. If nonofficial cover agents and operatives started to die, and Kittridge had not flashed a worldwide alert, not only would his career in government intelligence be over, he would likely have to contemplate a lifetime in federal prison. Those were the stakes. And if he had to dangle Ethan Hunt's mother from the tip of the Washington Monument, Kittridge would not hesitate to do so. By this time the next day, he would have to alert the president that Ethan Hunt was a mole code-named Job; and at that point, Kittridge could begin planning his retirement, if he was lucky.

When the phone rang in the communications room, Kittridge sat up alertly. This was not a relay line. The line ringing was a dedicated satellite channel, used only by field agents in specific emergencies.

"Yes," Kittridge said wearily.

"I see you've been out visiting the folks," Ethan Hunt said from London.

Kittridge waved a hand and everyone in the room immediately knew what was happening. He hit a mute button and yelled, "What do you need for a pinpoint?"

A technician clipped on a headset and turned a computer monitor toward the center of the room, checking the progress of the telephone tracing equipment. "Eighty seconds," the technician answered.

Kittridge nodded and released the mute button. "Been watching a little TV, have you?" he said evenly to Ethan.

"Hauling Mom off to jail in shackles was an especially nice touch."

The number 44 flashed on the computer screen.

The technician signaled to Kittridge to engage the mute button again, then said, "He's in England."

"Get MI-5!" Kittridge shouted to Barnes.

Kittridge returned to Ethan. "I want to reassure you that my first order of business, after you come in, is to get those ridiculous charges against your family dropped and eliminated completely from their files. Come in now, and we can plea-bargain down the charges against you as well."

The technician signaled, then said, "He's in London. Thirty seconds and I'll have a complete trace."

Kittridge checked the wall clock, then realized he was taking too much time to respond; he must not lose Hunt.

But Ethan came to the rescue. "Can I ask you something, Kittridge?"

"Certainly, Ethan, I wish you would."

"If you're dealing with someone who's crushed, stabbed, shot, and detonated five members of his own IMF team, how devastated do you think you're going to make him by marching Ma and Uncle Donald down to the county courthouse?"

Kittridge thought for a moment, wondering what chess game Hunt was playing. "I don't know, Ethan. Suppose you tell me."

Click.

Ethan was gone.

Kittridge looked hopefully at the technician, who shook his head. Harry Barnes checked the digital readout. "Lost him. We needed three more seconds. Just three damn seconds."

To most everyone's surprise, Kittridge smiled.

"We didn't lose him," he said, puzzled but not upset. "He wanted us to know he's in London."

Ethan checked the digital clock on the station's wall. A three-second buffer from a full trace was cutting it close, but he knew it had to be close in order for Kittridge to understand that the disconnect was timed and intentional. They were probably firing up the engines of an Air Force jet back at Andrews already, and by now Kittridge and Barnes most likely were in the CIA garage screeching toward daylight.

Deep in thought, Ethan turned to leave. Someone blocked his path. When Ethan looked up, he found Jim Phelps staring him in the face.

Ethan froze, eyes wide open in disbelief. An involuntary gasp shot out of Ethan's mouth as he fell backward against the phone booth.

Gaunt and pale, hunched over, Phelps was ravaged with exhaustion and pain.

But he was alive.

His hollow eyes looked into Ethan and through him. Phelps leaned against the wall, managing a small smile. His left arm was bandaged and hidden under a heavy overcoat, and a mound of bandages across his chest created a lump beneath the gray sweater he was wearing.

"You're a hard man to catch up with," Phelps said, his voice raw and weak.

Ethan just shook his head, staring.

"We need to go somewhere and sit down," Phelps said. "I'm not too good on my feet just now."

"I don't . . ." Ethan began to speak but stopped, uncertain of what he wanted to say. He kept staring at Phelps, who looked not unlike his ravaged appearance in Ethan's dream back in Prague. As he looked at Jim, the image of the gunshot and Jim falling into the river replayed in Ethan's brain. How could he have survived the bullet and the ice-cold water?

"We've got a lot to talk about," Phelps said, trying to bring Ethan back to the present. Phelps glanced around furtively. "And I expect we don't have a lot of time to do it in."

Ghost

THEY FOUND A PUB NEAR THE STATION, AND TOOK A TABLE in a corner, out of earshot from other patrons. Ethan needed several minutes to settle into the reality of Jim's presence, so Phelps just kept talking.

"When I got out of the river, I dumped my overcoat and hat in the water, because I knew they'd be dragging for me. I wanted time to figure some things out. The next day I managed to get some painkillers, got a nurse to bandage me up, then dragged myself to our safe house in Prague. Must've just missed you." He coughed and adjusted himself in the chair; Phelps was in obvious pain and couldn't get himself comfortable. "Anyway, I checked our aliases."

"And picked us up in the States," Ethan said, knowing the procedure Phelps followed.

He nodded. "But you weren't there long, were you?

You left before I could get there, and I could check just so many places."

"Yeah, smaller countries don't computerize customs records."

"So I watched Europe. Once you showed up in England, it was easy."

Ethan smiled. "You knew I liked the rentals at Liverpool Street."

"Hey, kid, I'm the one who showed them to you."

"I remember . . ." Ethan said, finally feeling like this conversation was real, and Jim Phelps was not another apparition, like the one he'd seen in the safe house in Prague.

"You followed me from the safe house here to the station."

Phelps nodded. "I didn't want to contact you right away because I was trying to track what had gone wrong. I needed to know that before I did anything else."

Ethan gathered himself and looked steadily into Jim's bloodshot eyes.

"Prague," Ethan said simply.

Phelps expelled a deep breath. "I knew something had gone to hell inside the IMF. But I didn't know what or who. I know it was bad not to tell you, but I just had to play it my way. I had to find out who the mole was. And I knew sooner or later something would draw him into the open. It turned out to be Prague."

"And I ignored the abort," Ethan said, looking away.

"I guess I should have told you more."

A stab of pain shot through Jim's body. He pulled a

bottle of painkillers from his pocket and downed two capsules.

Ethan leaned forward. "Jim, a doctor's got to look at that wound. You can't sit up straight."

"I can sit up straight. I just can't . . . sit up straight very well. It's not important right now! Listen to me, Ethan, by leaving the command post and calling the abort I flushed the mole." Jim coughed again, and grabbed the sleeve of Ethan's jacket. "I saw who shot me, Ethan. *I saw the mole.*"

Phelps was pale and losing strength by the second, propelled only by a fierce determination that, despite his weakened condition, suddenly brought life back to his watery eyes.

"It was Kittridge." Phelps pounded a fist on the table, spilling coffee from Ethan's cup. "Kittridge, Ethan."

Ethan stared at him, eyes widening. "Kittridge is the mole?"

Phelps nodded, his breathing labored. "Has to be."

"My God, Jim," Ethan said.

"Yeah," Phelps said, acknowledging the enormous implications of his revelation.

"Kittridge is Job."

Phelps coughed and nodded.

Ethan shook his head. "I don't understand. How did he do it?"

"I didn't understand, either," Phelps said, "but I've been doing nothing but thinking about it. Here it is. First, Kittridge killed Jack in the elevator. The override of the electronics was obviously a plant. Kittridge knows our electronics and he knew my mission design. That gave him control of Sarah and your exit, as well as Golitsyn's. He forced all of you out on the street, just where he wanted you."

Ethan's eyes bounced back and forth, reconstructing the scene, reliving the nightmare yet again, except this time he was more analytical, piecing together the scenario frame by frame.

"He overrode the elevator system from the beginning," Ethan said.

"Right. And once he got Jack, he knew I'd leave the command post. Then he came after me."

"He shot you on the bridge, I saw . . ."

"Right, he came out of the fog."

"But he must have had backup to take out Golitsyn and Sarah."

"Yeah."

"And Hannah?"

Jim hacked again; he looked like walking death. "Hannah made it back to the transfer vehicle, and Claire had already left after the abort."

"Yeah, but Kittridge couldn't have ID'd the vehicle and set the bomb by himself."

Jim shrugged helplessly. "I don't know who the backup was, but they were there."

"But why?" Ethan said. "Why Kittridge?"

Phelps went silent, brooding into his coffee. "When you think about it, Ethan, it was inevitable. No more Cold War. No more secrets you keep from everyone but yourself, operations where you answer to no one but yourself. Then one morning you wake up and find out the president of the United States is running the country—*without your permission*. The son of a bitch! How *dare* he? You realize it's over, you're an obsolete piece of hardware not worth upgrading,

171

you've got a lousy marriage and sixty-two grand a year. That was Kittridge's life. We'll go after that no-good son of a bitch, and—"

"We don't have to," Ethan said thoughtfully. "He'll come after us."

Jim sat back in his chair and looked at Ethan. "What's going to make him do that?"

"What he didn't get in Prague. The NOC list."

Jim was momentarily confused, then saw the certainty in Ethan's eyes. "Jesus, Ethan . . ."

"Yeah."

"How?"

"I just walked in and took it."

Jim stared at him.

"With a little help," Ethan added.

"Whoa. Good for you."

"And I set up a meeting tomorrow on the TGV, en route to Paris."

Phelps clicked into the picture, analyzing the train scenario; he nodded approvingly. "Tight security on that train. No guns. A real plus."

"Supposedly, if I deliver the NOC list to Max, Max has agreed to deliver Job to me. I'll have Claire and Luther Stickell with me on the train. Franz Kreiger will have helicopter transport waiting in Paris."

Jim looked quickly away, shaken at the mention of Claire's name.

Ethan read his face. "Jim . . ."

"Claire," Jim said simply.

"She . . ."

Phelps let out a sigh. "I was sitting in a café on Liverpool Street waiting for you and suddenly there she was, standing in the rain just outside the safe house, alive and beautiful, and thinking I'm dead and gone."

"She's devastated."

Jim's eyes were beginning to tear.

Ethan continued. "I wanted to keep her out of this. But she insisted on going after whoever killed you. I knew if I put her off, she'd do it on her own, and that would have been bad."

Phelps nodded. Then he said, "When I saw her I knew that you would take care of her."

The two friends and colleagues looked at each other. An awkward moment passed between them, as Ethan could read in Phelps's eyes the question of whether or not Ethan had already slept with Claire.

In fact, Phelps wondered if they'd slept together even before Phelps had "died." They'd been on many missions together, Ethan and Claire, all over the world. Phelps knew what it felt like for two people to work so closely in such difficult circumstances. A soldier once said to Phelps that the most exhilarating thing in life was to be shot at and missed. Claire and Ethan had been shot at several times, and missed. No doubt they'd shared the intense exhilaration of survival. What else had they shared? he asked himself.

"She's done better than could be expected," Ethan said, "probably better than me. But only because she wants revenge."

"God knows what she's had to do to forget about me and keep going," Jim said, looking out the window, "just keep going and get the job done. I . . ."

His voice broke off, as he fought a battle within

himself. "No," he said, "she can't know about me. No one can. Not until this is over. There's too much at stake."

Ethan thought about it. "You're probably right."

"I usually am," Jim said, trying to grin.

"Or maybe there's another way," Ethan suggested. "I could send her to you. Claire could take you to a doctor. Walk away from this. Let me handle it with Luther and Kreiger."

"Too much at stake," he repeated.

Ethan blew out some air, and looked into the eyes of Jim Phelps. IMF work had always been about life and death, but until recently the work hadn't exacted such a price from his soul as it was doing now. The missions he'd worked had been for good reasons, reasons he believed in. He knew who the bad guys were, and why the good guys should win.

Then Claire joined the team.

An extraordinary woman. And Jim's wife.

Nothing about the work had been as clear to Ethan since her arrival. Now especially, as he looked into the eyes of his old friend, mentor, boss.

"Once we leave the safe house," Ethan said to Jim, "you can go there and crash. Have a doctor come to you. And then I'll call you from Paris."

"Good," Jim said.

"And don't forget about the doctor," Ethan said, standing.

Jim nodded. "Good luck."

They shook hands.

Phelps felt something odd in Ethan's handshake. It wasn't quite as firm as usual.

Ethan left the pub and walked down the street back toward the safe house.

And as he walked, reflecting on the conversation he'd just had with Jim Phelps, he knew that his relationship with Jim, and Claire, was gone forever.

Ethan quietly ascended the stairs to the safe house apartment and unlocked the door. Luther was asleep in one room. Kreiger was God knows where, but would undoubtedly be ready to fly in the morning. Claire was, presumably, asleep in one of the bedrooms.

He went to the Powerbook, lifted the screen and saw a message prompt flashing. Pushed the retrieve button, and there was Max's confirmation. The train rendezvous was on.

Closing down the computer, he next went to the door to Claire's room and gently pushed it open.

The room was dark, but he could see that her bed was empty. And then he saw her sitting in a corner, an unlit cigarette in her mouth. She had a distant look on her face.

"What happened?" she asked.

"Max confirmed."

"Okay," she whispered, her voice a resignation. "Then tomorrow we go get Job."

"You don't have to be part of this," Ethan said.

"I don't?"

"No."

"Of course I do," she said evenly, looking at Ethan.

"No, you really don't," he repeated.

"Stop it, Ethan. You know that I do."

175

He took a deep breath in the quiet darkness of the room, and asked her, "Is this the only way?"

"Yes," Claire said, watching Ethan come over to her.

He knelt down next to her.

"Now I need to tell you something, and it's bad," Claire whispered, after a pause.

"Then don't tell me," Ethan whispered back.

"I have to say it."

"No, you don't."

"If I say it, then maybe it will go away."

"Okay, what is it?"

He was close enough to her that in the darkness they could see each other's eyes. She was looking at him as hard as she'd ever looked at anyone.

He wanted to kiss her. And if there was anything in life he should not do at this precise moment, Ethan knew, it was kiss Claire Phelps.

But that's what he did, knowing he would probably never do this again with her. Softly, then harder, with an urgency that seemed to pull all the heat from the atmosphere and place it between their lips. Ethan's head swirled and he knew if he kissed her a moment longer things would only get worse.

He pulled back and they looked at each other.

She whispered, "Do you know what I was going to say?"

"I think so."

She smiled sadly.

Still, Ethan found it to be a very beautiful smile.

Chunnel

AN MI-5 CHOPPER PICKED KITTRIDGE AND BARNES UP AT Heathrow and delivered them to a staging area near central London. Two CIA agents waited for them at the staging area, one of whom immediately handed Kittridge a small package, addressed simply FOR JOB.

"What the hell is this?"

"Incoming London office, sir, for you. X ray's clean. It's electronic but nonexplosive."

"That's comforting," Kittridge said, opening the small package at the top and pulling out two train tickets and a note that read: TGV/WATERLOO STATION/NOON.

He looked at his watch. Ten minutes to noon. Then something fell out of the package onto the grass helipad. Kittridge picked the item up and looked at it carefully, his eyes showing confusion but great interest.

It was a wrist-mounted Visco monitor.

Barnes waited for an explanation, but Kittridge gave none, slipping the tickets and Visco monitor into his jacket pocket.

"How long to Waterloo Station?" Kittridge asked one of the agents.

Two vans were waiting, motors running.

"Twenty, twenty-five minutes, depending on traffic."

"You've got ten," he shouted over the noise of the helicopter engines.

"Sir, that—"

"Ten minutes! Move!" Kittridge screamed, jogging for the vans.

One of the agents clicked a radio and notified London traffic control of their route, and the two vans screeched away from the helipad before the sliding side doors were even closed.

As Barnes buckled himself into a rear seat, he asked Kittridge how much backup he wanted on the TGV.

"Backup?" Kittridge snarled.

One of the London agents said, "I can have ten people there in five minutes."

Kittridge took a deep breath and looked at his colleagues.

"Do you understand we are dealing with a man who . . ." He caught himself and changed tack. "There is little doubt in my mind that Ethan Hunt will know it immediately if a dozen CIA agents board the train. I don't know if he is on the train, if he is planning to board the train elsewhere, or if he is planning to blow up the train once I'm on it. But it's just going to be Barnes and me boarding the train."

"We can have the train held if traffic is a problem," one of the agents said, as they hit a busy street.

"I don't want unusual, obvious activity around the train or our trip might be one big waste of time." He leaned forward to the driver. "Son, I want us to be there in ten minutes, and if I don't get what I want you'll be back in the Boy Scouts before the sun goes down."

The newest section of London's Waterloo Station was built to house the TGV, the high-speed train that consists of thirty cars. The famous Chunnel, popularly considered as one of the twentieth century's most significant engineering accomplishments, is composed of two shafts that were bored, at phenomenal expense, from England to France, and, of course, from France to England, meeting in the middle underneath the English Channel. One huge shaft contains two sets of tracks for two TGV trains running in opposite directions. The other, smaller shaft is a service tunnel used to house and transport machinery and electronics needed to keep the trains in good repair. Every facet of the Chunnel and its high-speed trains is monitored by a complex web of computer chip sensors and digital checkpoints. Brochures handed to first-time passengers explained that no one should be alarmed by the visible seepage of water on the Chunnel's bedrock walls; this was a natural occurrence and controlled by a series of automated pumps. The brochure was printed in fourteen languages, lest anyone be unsure as to how this marvel of modern engineering could keep the trillions of tons of seawater where they belonged.

The vans pulled up to a maintenance gate, and Kittridge's party ran down a cement corridor that led to the station proper. The visible half of the TGV itself gleamed like a polished bullet, and seemed to hover on its track, an earthbound rocket. The rear end of the train was actually another bullet-nosed engine; once the train arrived in the Gare du Nord in Paris, the rear became the front, and in this way the TGV could make its nonstop runs with maximum efficiency. Not a second wasted.

Passenger security screening was elaborate, much more so than Kittridge had seen anywhere in the States—of course, back in the States the IRA wasn't setting off bombs in railway stations just yet. Police X-rayed and inspected carry-on baggage, and scanned each passenger with metal detectors.

An MI-5 agent met the Americans and led them through an employee security gate and onto the train.

Most of the passengers on this particular TGV run were veterans of the train; as soon as the train departed Waterloo Station, out came the laptop computers and cellular phones.

Among those engaging cellular phones was Max, seated next to Matthias, who had a laptop computer booted up and waiting in front of him.

Max dialed a number to check the transmission quality. Satisfied with the signal, she handed it to Matthias.

"How long until we reach the Chunnel?" she asked him.

He checked his watch. "Twenty minutes."

"How soon into the Chunnel do we lose transmission ability?"

"Almost immediately," he said.

She frowned. "Then he'd better hurry, hadn't he?" she said, sitting back impatiently.

In a private sleeping compartment in the rearmost passenger car, a man drew the shades and placed two electronic appliances on the bed: a cellular phone and a boom box.

He unscrewed the speakers from the boom box and withdrew several items that were wrapped in a reflective foil created to pass through security X-ray machines. The foil packets were slit open and the dark components contained within fell to the mattress. When the components were assembled, the man held a pistol in his hand. From the second speaker he withdrew more packets, and from these he assembled a silencer.

Next he took a package of M&M's from his pocket, cut it open, and dumped four high-density plastic bullets on the mattress. These were lethal projectiles that expanded and corkscrewed upon impact with human flesh; two of these could eviscerate a person with split-second effectiveness—another time-saving development from the amoral world of espionage technology. The plastic bullets fit perfectly into the clip, which the man then shoved into his pistol. He chambered a round and screwed on the silencer, checked balance and aim, and slid the weapon into his jacket pocket.

He powered up his cellular, then sat down and lit a cigarette, taking a long, deep drag of smoke.

* * *

The train gathered speed on its way toward the limit of 150 mph, the sun-drenched countryside quickly becoming a green blur to the passengers. Max perused a copy of the *Financial Times,* but continually checked her watch.

Then her cellular phone emitted a beeping sound, and Matthias answered it.

"Yes?"

A few words came through, then he handed the phone to Max, whispering, "It's him."

Frowning, she took it. "This isn't what we discussed," she said, agitated. "You were to be here."

"My apologies," he replied, "but it couldn't be helped. There's a piece of black cloth under your seat. Tear it away and you'll find the disk."

She felt for the cloth packet. It was there. But she didn't remove it.

"Once again, I'm being asked to trust you," she said into the phone.

"And, once again, you should," he answered.

She looked at Matthias, thought a moment, then snatched the Velcro wallet from under the seat and handed it to her companion.

He opened it and withdrew a blue diskette, and immediately slid the diskette into the auxiliary drive of his laptop. One-half of his screen was already jammed with data under the heading of CRYPTONYM AND OPERATIONAL SPECS. The second half of the screen was blank. But then he activated the diskette, and the blank half of the screen came alive. The heading TRUE NAME appeared on top. Immediately, names, addresses, and identifiers popped into the blank space.

And a legend flashed in the center of the screen, bridging the two halves: IDENTITY MATCH.

Looking at the screen, Max couldn't contain her pleasure. She whispered into the phone, "Ha, dear boy! I do so hope this doesn't preclude a meeting in private."

"It doesn't, dear girl. As long as you tell me where the money is."

"The possibility alone is worth ten million," she replied. "Baggage car, rack three. Silver briefcase. Combination three-one-four."

"What about Job?"

"Oh," she said, "I wouldn't worry about him. Once you've got the money, he'll find you."

A click, and Ethan was gone.

Max leaned toward the laptop and watched the information download from the diskette to hard drive. She checked her watch.

"It's going as fast as it can," Matthias said, sensing her anxiety.

Claire sat in the third row from the front of a second-class car, facing the rear of the train. She was wearing a leather jacket and a plain dress, her hair pulled back. When she looked up and saw Eugene Kittridge and Harry Barnes approaching, she immediately turned away. They were working their way up the aisle, looking at each passenger carefully. Claire's heart began to pound as they drew closer.

A couple of people were coming the other way, so Kittridge and Barnes paused to let them pass.

"Only four more cars to go," Barnes said to his boss.

"And if we don't find him, we'll search the whole train again."

"So why did he choose the TGV?"

"High-speed train. No one gets on. No one gets off. High security. Perfect place for a pass-off to Max."

"But why tell us?" Barnes asked.

"He's putting on a show," Kittridge said, "I just don't know what kind."

The aisle cleared and the men continued.

Then a very fat man ambled through the door just behind Claire and started toward the rear of the car. Irritated, Kittridge and Barnes stood to the side to let the man pass. Claire took the opportunity to stand and follow the fat man, using him to shield herself from Kittridge and Barnes.

But Barnes caught a quick glimpse of her as she passed, and for a moment thought he'd just seen a woman who looked a lot like Claire Phelps. That, however, was impossible, he realized; she'd been blown into a thousand pieces in Prague. Kittridge was on the move again; Barnes knew that mentioning Claire Phelps would only irritate him.

Claire ducked into the doorway space between cars, and lifted the wrist monitor to her mouth.

"Ethan, Kittridge is on the train."

His response was slow and quiet. "Kittridge is Job. Max delivered. How far is he from Luther?"

She looked up at the placard above the exit identifying this as car 19. "Two cars," she said. "Where are you?"

"Close. You are my eyes, Claire. Stay with Kittridge."

She adjusted the hat she was wearing, and went down the aisle after Kittridge and Barnes.

Max watched intently as the computer screen flashed a LIST COMPLETE prompt. She immediately dialed a number into her cellular. When the call was answered, she said simply, "He's in the baggage car."

"I'll be there," the man in the sleeping compartment replied, clicking off the line. He then rechecked the fitting of the silencer of his gun, slid it into his jacket, took a final puff of his cigarette, and left the compartment.

Matthias took Max's cellular phone, attached it to a PCMIA fax-modem card, and plugged it into the laptop computer. He dialed a preprogrammed number that elicited a dial tone but then disengaged with a MODEM DENIED prompt.

Matthias was confused.

"Well, what's the problem?" Max asked.

"Connection denied."

"Try it again."

"It's trying automatically. But it's not working," Matthias said.

"Is it the phone or the computer?"

The computer dialed again, and again was denied access to the modem.

"Are the batteries down?" Max asked, with growing alarm.

"Everything's fresh."

"Run diagnostics," she said.

"I'm running them," Matthias said, staring at his Powerbook's screen. "This machine is perfect. The fax program is enabled. The modem is configured. And we know the phone works. But it's not transmitting."

Several seats away, Luther Stickell poked his head up to peek at Max and Matthias. The consternation he saw on their faces told him what he needed to know, that the jamming signal emitting from the specially formatted Nokia phone that sat on the service tray in front of him was functioning properly.

Matthias refit his connections and tried the modem. Again, the cellular wouldn't transfer the call.

He lifted up slightly in his seat and looked around the passenger car.

"What?" Max asked.

Half a dozen other people were making calls, another half dozen worked on laptop computers.

Luther Stickell was dressed in a gray suit, and looked very much the traveling businessman. He worked at his own laptop, making certain the antennae of his Nokia was aimed in Max's direction.

"I don't know," Matthias said. "I thought maybe we were being jammed. But everyone else seems to be working fine."

"Reboot the computer," she said angrily. "And if it doesn't work, we'll use somebody else's."

"I'm not seeing anything but civilians," Harry Barnes said to Kittridge, as they neared the car Max, Matthias, and Luther were riding in.

"This is beginning to feel like bullshit," Kittridge said. "It would help if we knew what Max looked like."

"Maybe we don't have to," Barnes said, looking

forward. "If Hunt passed off the disk, Max is going to want to check it. We should be looking for laptops."

Kittridge nodded.

Ahead, Luther saw Kittridge and Barnes approaching. They would know Luther on sight. He immediately slapped his laptop shut, positioned his Nokia phone so that it remained aimed at Max, then left his seat and headed in a hurry for the rear of the car.

Unfortunately, an alert waiter spotted Luther leaving, noticed the cellular phone he'd left behind, and went to assist him.

"Excuse me, sir," the waiter said, snatching up the phone and catching Luther. "Your telephone."

As the waiter approached Luther with the phone, passengers that he passed were suddenly disconnected from calls.

Matthias, having rebooted his computer and re-enabled its fax modem, tried again. This time, with Luther's Nokia phone out of range, the call went through, and the computer screen flashed TRANSFER IN PROGRESS.

"It's working," Matthias said, the weight of the world falling away from his face.

Max checked her watch.

"We've got five minutes to the Chunnel," she said.

There was nothing Matthias could do to make the computer go faster; he could only stare and hope.

Luther exited the car, hurried through the executive and club cars, then locked himself into a bathroom, not bothering to look if he'd been spotted or followed; he just wanted out of there. He set the laptop and phone down on the stainless steel vanity, then looked in the mirror. Perspiration streamed down his face, soaking the stiffly starched white collar of his shirt. He breathed heavily.

Luther Stickell was a wreck. He was used to being tucked away in an electronic cottage, out of the line of fire, so to speak. But now with Kittridge and Barnes and who knows who else bearing down on him, Stickell was panicking.

Someone tried the bathroom door. It was locked. Then the door shook hard. Nobody had to use the john that badly. Somebody knew he was in there.

And it wasn't Kittridge or Barnes, who were still in the business car that Luther had just vacated. They looked at Max and at half a dozen other business-people, all using laptops.

Max instantly smelled CIA as the men approached. But her demeanor didn't change; if anything, it softened. She sipped her coffee, read the *Times*, and exchanged a few pleasantries with Matthias.

Kittridge and Matthias passed them by.

Claire Phelps paused in one of the walk spaces between cars, as her wrist monitor signaled incoming. It was Ethan whispering into her earpiece.

"I've got the money," he said. "Meet me in the baggage car. Now."

In order to get to the baggage car she would have to pass Kittridge and Barnes. She lowered her head, and walked briskly down the aisle, turning away as she passed the two of them.

Claire flew through the last executive car and headed for the coach car.

But this time, Barnes was certain he'd recognized Claire. He knew Kittridge would probably have him decommissioned for the thought, but he didn't care.

Barnes grabbed Kittridge by the elbow.

"Believe me or not, but I'm telling you that was Claire Phelps who just walked past us."

To Barnes's surprise, Kittridge reacted with great interest, and urgency.

"Let's go," he said, motioning Barnes to give chase.

They caught a glimpse of Claire disappearing into the club car, but by the time they got there, she was gone. They went to the bathroom and tried the door.

It was locked.

"Get this open," Kittridge said to Barnes.

Barnes pulled what looked like a stainless steel nail file from his pocket, and quickly picked the bathroom door's lock. The men stood on either side of it as it fell open.

The bathroom looked empty.

But there was no window, no place for anybody to go.

Barnes tentatively poked his head inside and at that moment Luther Stickell came dropping down from his wedged position over the doorway, slamming his laptop computer toward Barnes. Luther was a brilliant tech op. Fighting, however, was not on his list of specialties. Not even in the top ten.

Barnes subdued him in three seconds.

Kittridge leaned wearily in the door frame.

"Hello, Luther," he said. "Where's Hunt?"

"Mr. Kittridge," Luther said, the perspiration falling off his face like rain from a windowpane, "the NOC list is being downloaded from a computer on this train. Right now."

"Where?"

*   *   *

Claire picked the lock to the baggage car and slipped inside.

It was dark and cool in there, and she took a moment to adjust to the low light. Then she saw the profile of Jim Phelps, ten feet away.

He was seated on a suitcase in a rear corner of the car, his face lined with shadows from a storage rack. His head was tilted downward, a pensive look upon his face.

"Ethan's on his way," Claire said quickly to her husband, "he's got to be right behind me. Listen to me, Jim. Is it such a good idea to kill him? We take the money. Ethan takes the blame. No one else has seen you alive. No one will believe his story."

Jim looked at her for several moments, choosing to remain in the shadows.

He took a deep breath, then reached to rub the side of his neck.

But something strange was happening to his face. Jim's right hand seemed to disappear into the flesh below an ear. Then his features became distorted, and suddenly, to her horror, Claire realized Jim's face was a mask. And it was being worn by Ethan Hunt.

Peeling away the latex strips still on his face, Ethan said, "Of course, I'm sorry to hear you say that, Claire."

She stepped forward, shaking her head.

"Ethan?"

And then the real Jim Phelps spoke up.

"Yes. Ethan Hunt, darling. Remember him?"

Jim Phelps stepped forward from the shadows on the other side of the baggage car. He held the 9mm gun smuggled aboard the train in his radio, which he had then assembled in the sleeping compartment. Phelps was dressed in a black nylon skydiver's suit; he had an equipment pack belted to his hip. And his sickly demeanor of the previous day had disappeared. He stood ramrod straight, looking fit and alert. No bandages, no injuries. Just the gun.

Claire looked from Jim to Ethan, who remained seated on the suitcase.

Ethan seemed not at all surprised to see Jim.

"You knew about Jim?" Claire asked.

Phelps answered for him. "Of course he did. Just exactly *when* he knew is something of a question. Before or after I showed up in London—mind telling me, Ethan?"

Ethan looked at Jim with deadly calm, having spent the night thinking about Jim's betrayal and wondering about Claire's complicity.

"Before London. But after you took the Bible out of the Drake Hotel in Chicago."

"They stamped it, didn't they?" Jim said. "Those damn Gideons."

Jim's wristwatch emitted a series of tiny beeps. "Two minutes before Kreiger shows up," he said, then turned to Ethan. "So this will have to be quicker than I'd like. Certainly quicker than you'd like."

Claire stared at Ethan.

"Ethan, if you knew about Jim, why did you . . . ?"

Jim cut in again. "Why the masquerade? Why take the risk?" He laughed bitterly. "Claire, you've asked the question and you are the answer." Phelps looked at Claire with no affection in his eyes, just a brooding anger that gave him a demented glint neither Ethan nor Claire had witnessed before.

Ethan nodded to Claire. "I knew about Jim."

"But," Jim said to his wife, "he didn't know about you. That's what kept him going. That's what he was truly curious about."

Then he faced Ethan. "In all fairness, Ethan, Claire was never convinced her charms would work with you. But I was supremely confident, having tasted the goods. 'Thou shalt not covet thy neighbor's wife,' Ethan." Phelps snapped his attention back to Claire. "Oh, Ethan is in love with you, Claire, make no mistake about it. And like all the world's lovers, he's tortured by the one same pathetic question . . . 'Does she feel the same way I do?' " He let the thought hang in the air, the train clicking below them. "Well, Claire, do you? Have you been exploiting Ethan's feelings, or returning them?"

Ethan spoke up. "Nothing happened between us. I won't say it wasn't on my mind. But nothing happened."

Claire looked steadily from Ethan toward her husband and said in a businesslike voice, "Jim, let's just get the money and get out of here." Then she turned to Ethan. "The money, Ethan. Right now."

Phelps didn't like the calm Ethan was maintaining, because it resembled Ethan's demeanor during a mission. As far as he knew, Phelps was holding all the cards at the moment. But Ethan either didn't think so, or had resigned himself to the situation and didn't care anymore.

Ethan handed Claire a sheaf of bearer bonds. Max had been true to her word, at least on that matter: ten one-million-dollar bonds, coupons attached.

"You've earned it," Ethan said to Claire.

"Count it," Jim said.

Claire started to check the bonds.

"Tell me something, Claire," Ethan said. "That night in Prague, was it you or Jim who blew up the car and scattered Hannah all over town?"

"Keep counting, Claire," Phelps said.

"It was me," she said, averting her eyes. "I did it."

"Satisfied?" Phelps asked.

"All ten million," Claire answered, her voice growing very quiet.

"Fold it. Fold it tight," Jim said.

"Aren't you going to thank me, Jim?" Ethan said. "Ten million is better than six."

"Don't flatter yourself. Six was for Eastern Europe. You made a lousy deal. Ten for the world list? What is that? But I needed you for the transfer with Max. I got a little extra change; and you got a little, too."

Again, his watch alarm beeped.

"Sorry, Ethan. I really am. Time's up," Phelps said. "Say good-bye."

He raised the gun.

"You're wrong about one thing," Ethan said. "I'm not the only one who has seen you alive."

Ethan held up one hand to show that he did not hold a weapon, then leaned forward to display a pair of eyeglasses hanging from his pocket. He tossed them to Jim Phelps.

Phelps snatched them out of the air and looked at them with growing disbelief. They were Visco glasses. And from the tiny microspeaker came a familiar voice, that of Eugene Kittridge.

"Good morning, Mr. Phelps," Kittridge said, from somewhere on the train, where he watched the Visco wrist monitor Ethan had had delivered to him with the train tickets at the London helipad.

Phelps and Claire were stunned.

"You son of a bitch," Phelps said, pointing the gun.

"Don't, Jim," Claire said quickly, her voice trembling now. "It's over."

"Now we don't have to eliminate him? You like that idea, don't you, Claire? Don't you?" Phelps's voice took on a burning edge.

But Claire nodded. "Yes."

"Jim," Ethan said calmly. "She's right. It's over."

Ethan stood and took a step toward Phelps.

"Ethan, I've always taught you, nothing can be more dangerous than the truth. It can kill you." Phelps's face was twisted with rage.

With a lightning-quick move, Phelps shifted his aim and fired a bullet straight into Claire.

Ethan dove for him and knocked his arm as the next shot was fired. The gun went skidding away. Phelps's watch beeped suddenly. The hesitation that sound caused was all Phelps needed to pound a knee into Ethan's stomach and knock him back with an elbow to the head. Dazed, Ethan hit the ground. Phelps grabbed the envelope with the bonds, then fled the baggage car.

Ethan gasped for air and crawled over to Claire.

She was still alive. Her breath was short and raspy. But she was alive.

He looked in the dim light for her wound, then found it in her chest. He couldn't help but think about the drug they had used in Kiev to simulate death, when they had fooled the corrupt Russian politician.

And afterward he had cradled her face in his hands and watched the consciousness return to her eyes. She had been so happy to see him in that strangely tender moment, almost as though it had been Ethan, and not the chemical antidote, that brought her back to life.

But this bullet wound was not going to be repaired. He knew what kind of bullet Jim had used, and he knew the massive internal damage it was designed to inflict. "Claire . . ." he said.

She lifted a hand and felt her chest. And then she, too, knew the extent of the damage.

"This stuff is so sticky," Claire said, of the blood that now covered her fingers.

"Claire."

"It's all right, Ethan," she said, "you'll bring me back . . . won't you . . ."

He touched her hair. "I always have, Claire."

Her eyes closed, and her breathing stopped.

Ethan held her for a moment, then gently set her head down on the floor.

When Phelps first introduced Ethan to Claire, Ethan had taken one look at her and knew things between them would end badly. How could it be any other way? Jim was his boss and friend. Claire was Jim's wife. Ethan had fallen in love with her almost instantly. And he knew that she felt something clear and strong for him. It could only end badly.

And it had.

Should he have just walked away from Claire and the IMF two years ago? he asked himself. Maybe. Probably. But what would have been the point? She would have been there, in his thoughts and feelings, haunting him. Being with her for two years, trying to mask his feelings, had hurt, but leaving would have hurt worse.

Now Claire lay dead beneath him.

It was not his fault, but what did fault matter at this moment? Jim shot her, but she was as much Ethan's loss as his.

Ethan had exposed Jim to Kittridge through the use of the Visco glasses; he had proven his innocence, and left it to Kittridge to stop Max's transfer of the NOC list. Mission accomplished.

But so what? he thought.

So what?

Claire lay dead in his arms. Ethan felt cheated of his respect for Phelps and cheated of his feelings for Claire.

But what was there to do about any of it?

Right now just one thing: complete the mission.

Jim Phelps had escaped.

Up

WHEN ETHAN STAGGERED TO HIS FEET, HE REALIZED THAT Phelps had left the baggage car through the rear door. To go where? There was only the other engine car, which at the moment served as the train's caboose. But the train was traveling at 100 mph by now, on its way shortly to 150 mph; Phelps was not about to leap off. Kittridge and Barnes no doubt had notified authorities to surround the train the moment it stopped, so Phelps wasn't going to be able to hide. Ethan knew, however, that Jim Phelps wouldn't have set foot on this train without a carefully conceived escape plan. Actually, two escape plans. One for a successful transfer of the NOC list to Max, the murder of Ethan, and a quick exit, bearer bonds in hand, in Paris. Plan B, no doubt, was the disaster scenario, put in place only if something had gone terribly wrong on the train. And something had: Ethan's use of the Visco glasses to expose Jim. Given the circumstances, Phelps would be on to Plan B by now. And Plan B could only involve getting off the train while it was still in motion. The beeping watch and Phelps's concern about a rendezvous with Kreiger told Ethan what the escape plan had to be, but he still found it hard to accept.

He ran to the rear of the car, and in the transition area between the baggage car and the rear engine car, Ethan found his answer. There was a metal maintenance ladder near the door of the engine car, leading to a hatch and the roof of the train.

And there at the top of the ladder was Jim Phelps.

Phelps had slipped a pair of plastic goggles over his eyes, and held the same kind of magnetic climbing cups Ethan and Kreiger had used to crawl through the ducts at Langley.

Ethan took two steps and leaped upward. Jim caught him with a boot to the side of the head, knocking Ethan back to the floor. By the time Ethan scrambled to his feet and started for the ladder, Jim was up and out of the hatch. Ethan climbed up the ladder, battling the hot wind whipping in from the open hatch. He poked his head into the clear, and saw Phelps a few yards away, crawling on his belly, dragging himself with the suction cups toward the end of the engine, which sloped sharply down as it reached the engineer's windows. Crawling against the wind was a slow, arduous process, but Phelps edged relentlessly along the gleaming metal roof of the train.

The wind roared in Ethan's ears and tried to tear the clothing right off his body. But he slid onto the roof and held on by grabbing small wind baffles that ran the length of the train.

When Phelps looked back and saw Ethan climbing out after him, he could hardly believe it. He screamed something in Ethan's direction but the roar of the wind and the train was deafening.

As the train came to a slight bend in the tracks, the momentum swung Ethan to the side, the wind got under him and flipped him over, so that he ended up facing the opposite direction of Phelps. He battled to hold on.

Phelps reached the end of the train, by pulling out and replanting his suction cups, then pulled a large metal clip from his leg pack and hooked it to his belt.

Ethan watched, barely holding on.

Then out of the distance behind the train a small black dot started growing larger, closing quickly.

It was a helicopter.

Kreiger.

Phelps waved an arm to signal him, and then the final piece of the puzzle fell into place for Ethan. It confirmed for Ethan that it had been Kreiger who killed Golitsyn and Sarah, then was "recruited" by Claire to help them break into Langley and retrieve the NOC list. It had all been part of Jim's setup. And now Kreiger was closing in on the train, dangling a metal cable with a hook on it, prepared to perform a midair rescue for Jim Phelps. Looking over his shoulder, in the distance Phelps saw the tunnel leading down to the Chunnel beneath the English Channel, and he waved frantically to Kreiger to swoop in for the snatch-and-grab.

Ethan suddenly lost his grip and slid several yards

down the car, catching one of the baffles at the last moment.

The helicopter lowered down, and Kreiger guided a weighted cable down toward Phelps. Phelps needed to grab the hook on the end of the cable and clip it to his belt, and the second he did he would be a free man. But in the fierce wind the cable dangled back and forth, and Kreiger flew in wide arcs to keep his craft stable as he chased the screaming train.

Kreiger, seeing the mouth of the Chunnel approaching all too quickly, frantically signaled Phelps to go for the cable, and flew directly over the rear engine to try to angle the cable into position. Finally, Phelps got hold of the cable and was about to hook on, when Ethan went for a do-or-die maneuver. He let go of his hold on the wind baffles; the force of the wind blew him across the top of the car and directly at Phelps. He slid into Phelps's legs and pulled him back down to the roof, grabbing the cable out of his hand and jamming the hook into an open baffle. The helicopter, to Kreiger's horror, was now hooked to the rear of the train. Phelps struggled with Ethan to release the cable, but Ethan fought him furiously.

Kreiger had seconds before slamming into the top of the tunnel, so he pulled back on his controls and fought to bring his helicopter back under control. Ethan and Jim were both holding on to the same suction cup with one hand and fighting with the other. They saw the terror on Kreiger's face, looked forward in time to see the tunnel's opening, and flattened themselves against the engine's roof as the train screamed into the Chunnel.

At the last possible second Kreiger veered the

minicopter down and barely avoided the walls of the tunnel. He might be a duplicitous murderer, but Kreiger was one hell of a pilot—the man was navigating a chopper inside the Chunnel.

The tug of the chopper on the train had set off an alarm in the front engine, and the engineer radioed back to his rear engine conductor. No answer. He called a security guard stationed in the last passenger car. When the guard ran to the rear engine, he found the conductor dead in the compartment, an earlier victim of Jim Phelps. Then he looked up and with total surprise and horror saw a helicopter tethered to the rear of the train, its bearded pilot jamming the craft forward. When he radioed his frantic report to the engineer, he was met with disbelief.

"I'm looking at it," the security guard screamed into the phone. "Accelerate the train or it'll crash directly into us!"

The engineer pushed his throttle, and with the lurch of speed, Phelps began to lose hold of his grip on the suction cup, and gradually slid down the face of the engine's Plexiglas window, an inexorable slide toward what would be a pounding death. But Ethan pulled himself up to the center of the roof and lowered a hand toward the weakening Phelps. Jim clawed for Ethan's outstretched hand, and managed a gymnast's grip on Ethan's wrist. The veins bulged in Ethan's throat and forehead as he dragged Phelps up toward the roof of the train. Phelps looked like he was ready to die from exhaustion when he got back up to the level part of the roof, but with a suddenness that caught Ethan off guard, he whipped a punch into Ethan's face, and knocked loose his grip on the suction cup. Ethan slid toward the side of the car and managed to grab the other suction cup before falling off the edge, but his legs flailed in the air as he tried to regain balance.

Seeing Ethan's predicament, Kreiger motioned for Phelps to make a move, using hand gestures to indicate he wanted Jim to slide down the nose of the engine to get low enough for a jump to one of the helicopter's landing skids. There was no room for error, but Phelps knew if he didn't do something soon, he'd simply lose control and fall to his death.

Inside the tunnel, the barrage of noise was excruciating, wind from the train howling like a tropical storm, the helicopter's engine whining from the strain of the maneuvers.

Kreiger brought the chopper forward so that it touched the tip of the train's rear engine. Taking what he hoped wasn't his final deep breath, Phelps let go of the suction cup, slid down the windows, and held on to the baseball-bat-sized windshield wipers on the surface. The cable dipped and bobbed as Kreiger fought the chopper in the darkness of the tunnel, trying to bring the chopper's skids within Phelps's reach. Jim rose up and stretched an arm toward the left skid.

It was at that moment that the other TGV, the twin of this one, heading from Paris to London, screamed past. Kreiger lurched the chopper upward, and Phelps missed the skid and fell backward, his body clinging to the engine's windshield in a wide spread eagle. Then Kreiger's chopper pitched nose down, and swooshed to the left. Kreiger brought it forward, closer to the train at a slight angle, trying to use his rotor blades in an attempt to chop Ethan Hunt into pieces. But one of the blades nicked a chunk of tunnel, and sparks exploded in every direction. A completely crazed look in his eyes, Kreiger righted the craft and went once more for Jim. The ten million dollars was summoning courage from within Kreiger that even he didn't know existed.

Jim pushed himself up and away from the window yet again, desperately reaching for one of the chopper's skids. It dipped toward his hand, and this time Jim got hold of it, threw a leg up, and tossed himself onto the skid. He righted himself and stood on the skid, checking Ethan's position. The extra weight of Phelps lowered the chopper, and Ethan had a split-second calculation to make; a wrong answer meant an instant end to this life. He was momentarily aligned with the other skid, so he let go of the train and leaped for the skid, grabbing hold and pulling himself up. Now Ethan and Phelps were each on a skid, riding just below and on the other side of Kreiger's cockpit. Kreiger arced the copter, trying to dump Ethan, but there just wasn't room inside the tunnel to maneuver. And Ethan didn't plan to stay there long, anyway. He reached into his pocket and pulled out a stick of Jack's magic gum. The wind ripped the paper off, exposing the telltale red-and-green message to Phelps.

Phelps didn't miss it. Behind his goggles, his eyes became huge. He screamed to Kreiger, who could hear nothing, so Jim motioned for a gun, and Kreiger reached for a Browning under his seat.

Ethan mashed the gum together and slapped it firmly to the chopper's underbelly.

Jim swung himself down and kicked at it, while

Ethan went into a squat, gauging a leap back to the train. But Kreiger was letting the copter fall back. No way Ethan could make the jump. And no way he could do anything *but* jump, unless he wanted to explode with the chopper.

The gum detonated just as Ethan launched himself in what should have been a futile jump. But the concussion of the explosion gave him the extra thrust he needed: with a rib-pounding thud he splatted against the TGV's windshield and clung there. The explosion ripped open the belly of the chopper, causing it to wobble badly to the left, its blades pounding off the tunnel wall, breaking themselves to pieces. What was left of the damaged chopper nose-dived and exploded in a ball of fire and twisted metal. Ethan used one arm to cover his head, but felt sharp slivers of shrapnel slash into his legs and back. With the explosion, the train's engineer pressed emergency stop buttons, and the high-tech braking system was slowing the train with remarkable efficiency. The only problem for Ethan was that the skeleton of the chopper was rolling and bouncing forward at a much greater speed than the train was stopping, and half a rotor was still turning wildly. As the train came to a stop the chopper bounced off the tunnel and turned toward the engine, the rotor whipping around toward Ethan's head like a buzz saw. The final turn of the rotor died about four inches from Ethan's face.

Ethan's ears were still roaring with sound, even though the tunnel had taken on a sudden, eerie quiet, as the great train came to a stop somewhere beneath the English Channel.

* * *

Minutes before, when the TGV had first slid into the tunnel, Max reacted to a curse from Matthias. He gestured to the screen that showed them a terrible message:

connection terminated
transfer lost

"We're going to have to do this all over again when we get out of the tunnel?" she asked Matthias.

"No," he said soberly.

She looked at him.

He was watching the screen, which was suddenly awash with scrambled data.

"The program is written to delete itself if a transfer is interrupted without a proper terminating sequence. It's written for one download, and then it eats itself alive. We didn't get that far."

Max let out a deep breath of disgust.

"Job will have to make this right," she said to Matthias. "I suggest you go speak with him."

"How about talking to me instead?" a voice from behind them said.

Max and Matthias turned around to see Eugene Kittridge, with Harry Barnes and Luther Stickell right with him.

"Computers are a bitch," Luther said to Matthias.

Max sized up the trio, then edged over to the empty seat next to her, gesturing for Kittridge to sit down. Max seemed at ease with the situation.

"My lawyers will have a field day with this," she said brightly. "Entrapment, jurisdictional conflicts . . ."

Kittridge leaned forward, bringing his voice down to a polite murmur. "Maybe we'll just keep the courts out of this one."

She nodded. "I'm quite sure we can find something I have that you need."

He matched her smile. "You know," he said, "I'd love to try."

Barnes looked at Kittridge, and saw a man who for the first time in two years looked happy and relaxed. Which annoyed Barnes. The NOC list was protected; Kittridge would extract, no doubt, a passel of valuable intelligence from Max in exchange for letting her walk from this transaction; the molehunt had flushed Jim Phelps. All of those things made Kittridge quite content.

Yet he did not know if Ethan Hunt—the person who had made all of this good news possible—was dead or alive. And, Barnes observed, Kittridge didn't seem to care.

Hunt was IMF, meaning that staying alive was his responsibility, and his alone.

Paris

For THREE RESTLESS DAYS IN A LONDON HOSPITAL, ETHAN thought about little other than Jim and Claire.

Why had Jim allowed so much loss of life in pursuit of his dark goal? Jack, Sarah, Hannah, even Claire. Did staying in the IMF for thirty years make human life as dispensable to Jim as a forged passport? Certain questions were going to go unanswered—Jim was dead, and his secrets went with him. Only by staying in the IMF himself would Ethan gain a deeper understanding of Jim Phelps. But for Ethan, staying in the IMF was out of the question.

Sorting out his feelings for Claire proved more complicated than thinking about Jim.

In violation of IMF policy, Ethan left the hospital and flew to Paris to attend Claire's funeral. She was survived by both parents, an older sister, and an older brother. The family had been told Claire died while attempting to foil a robbery—they thought she was an Interpol investigative agent—and the family was presented with a posthumous award for Claire in recognition of her heroism during the botched robbery; awards tended to make family members refrain from asking delicate questions. They would never know that their daughter had been a willing participant in an attempt to broker the NOC list and disappear with ten million dollars. Had she been successful with Phelps in his plan, perhaps she would never have seen her family again, vanishing to a remote, luxurious life in Brazil or Fiji. More questions that would never be answered. Judging by the palpable sadness that pervaded all of Claire's family members, Ethan sensed they knew nothing of her double life, and most likely never would. And that was best all around. They would certainly never hear anything of Claire's double life from Ethan, since he'd never met them, and couldn't. Ethan's contacting Claire's family would put them at risk and probably only deepen their emotional wounds. Anyway, for all he knew, these people might be plants, sent by Kittridge to mislead anyone who did have knowledge of Claire's background. Who knew at this point what the truth was?

He observed the funeral from a distance, then at the cemetery stood on a grassy knoll fifty yards from the grave, allowing a warm, silent, spring rain to wash his uncovered head and face.

Unnoticed, he watched the tiny party of mourners listen to a reading at the graveside. All the while, Ethan wondered what he was doing there at all. Claire had asked Jim not to kill Ethan, but had been perfectly prepared to leave with Phelps and never see Ethan again. He wondered what she might have done next, had she lived. Maybe she would have killed Jim and kept the money for herself. Maybe, months later, she would have contacted Ethan and tried to repair the damage. All the maybes in the world weren't going to change what happened.

From the very second Jim Phelps had called the abort in Prague, Ethan had sensed something was wrong, beyond just a failed mission. Jim had been too insistent, too clear in the midst of an unclear situation. Then there was Kreiger's knife that fell into the computer room at Langley, a knife similar to the one used to kill Sarah. There was the Bible from the Drake Hotel, and Phelps suddenly turning up in London, with answers to all of Ethan's questions about the Prague mission, answers to questions Ethan hadn't even had time to ask him. Jim Phelps was thorough, Ethan would give him that. And Claire's kiss back in the London safe house flat. There was heat in it, also a sadness and a finality that he hadn't conjured up on his own. Claire's heart revealed its betrayal long before her mind had.

It was difficult for Ethan to know that in his own heart he still loved Claire. Yet that's what he felt. Even knowing that she participated in the deaths of his colleagues and friends, he still felt something deep and primal for her. Somehow he ascribed her evil deeds to the amoral influence of Jim Phelps. At least, he did for now, trying to hold on to that moment a few nights ago when they'd kissed in the train compartment, after meeting with Kreiger and Luther. That was when their lips had accidentally brushed, then drew together out of pure force of feeling. He would never admit to anyone how good that moment felt. There were so many things about Ethan Hunt's life that he would not, and could not, reveal to anyone else.

What did it mean, Ethan wondered, as Claire's body was lowered into the wet earth, that he could love someone who betrayed everything and anything he valued?

Of course, in truth, he knew exactly what it meant.

It meant that matters of the heart supersede morality.

When the heart is involved, things happen because they *have* to happen, regardless of consequences.

That was the oldest truth of all in a world filled with lies.

Your Mission, Mr. Hunt

IT RAINED THE ENTIRE DAY IN PARIS AND WELL INTO THE night. Most of that afternoon and evening after Claire's funeral Ethan walked the streets of Paris, watching people shop in the small food markets, fall into cafés for an espresso and a cigarette, browse magazine stands, or stroll arm-in-arm with friends. Ethan walked the streets for hours, despite the pains in his body; he wanted to see people living normal lives, see them making decisions that did not involve life or death, nothing more significant than choosing red wine or white wine, meat or fish. He stopped in student cafés just to hear the sound of passionate conversations, and laughter, the pulse of everyday life.

As the evening grew late he walked to the Trocadero plaza and viewed the lights of the city and the Eiffel

Tower. Then he took a side street that he knew was hundreds of years old. The stones of this street had survived plagues, world wars, Nazis, even rap music. The same stones would be there, quite likely, long after Ethan was dead. It felt good to put his feet on something permanent and solid.

In the morning he caught a flight to Heathrow, where he met up with Luther Stickell in a small pub. Both were booked on flights to the States, though with different routings. Luther was bound for JFK, then Washington and Langley; Ethan was headed for Chicago's O'Hare, then on to Madison, Wisconsin, and home.

They ordered a couple of Watney's.

Luther pointed to a television set over the bar. During a summary of the week's news, CNN replayed footage from the dramatic helicopter-in-the-Chunnel wreck. It had been determined to be the work of a lone, crazed man intent on suicide. There was no mention of men fighting on the rear engine. No mention of a dead woman in the baggage car. No mention of an arms dealer on board making a deal with the CIA.

In fact, it was mentioned that there were, quite miraculously, no injuries or disturbances at all on the train. Just a nut in a helicopter chasing the TGV and crashing.

"Talk to your folks?" Luther asked Ethan, as the waitress set the ales down.

Ethan took a sip and nodded.

"So how're they feeling?"

"About what?"

"The official apology from the Justice Department,

cash settlement in the amount of one hundred and twenty-seven thousand dollars in lieu of false arrest, VIP treatment, the whole nine yards."

"Well, my mother was a little confused about how federal agents could mistake her and Uncle Donald for a couple of dope smugglers in the Florida Keys."

Luther laughed and clinked glasses with Ethan.

"Uncle Donald is still pretty unhappy," Ethan continued. "He's not surprised that the government screwed up, that part he kind of takes for granted. He just can't believe that the president himself hasn't called to apologize."

"Oh, yeah?"

"I told him not to hold his breath. Just chalk it all up as another sign of the decline of Western civilization."

"He'd probably rather hear that from the president."

"Exactly what he said to me. Maybe he'll settle for Oprah."

Ethan offered another toast. "Here's to you, Luther." They clinked glasses. "To being off the disavowed list."

They drank again. "Hey, man," Luther said, smiling, "I'm the flavor of the month now."

"You're more than that, Luther. They were mistaken about you and they're trying to show you they know it. They want you back in."

"Sure. They want me back in so I don't *break* in. They still can't figure out how we did it."

"You didn't tell them at your debriefing?"

"Why waste it? I figured I'd let them reinstate my back pay, give me a promotion, I'd check out my office at Langley, and *then*, assuming I'm still in a good mood, maybe, just maybe, we'll talk about it."

Ethan laughed. "That's right, you'll be walking through the HQ and tech ops will be poking their heads out of offices to get a peek at you. The legend returns."

"Oh, yeah, and don't think I'm not going to do it, too. If Kittridge doesn't think he'll have to do some soft shoe for me, then that man's dreaming."

The two friends laughed and ordered another round.

"The whole business," Ethan said, "it's all one big negotiation, isn't it?"

Luther looked reflective for a moment.

"Ethan, why don't you come back with me?"

He wagged his head slowly. "I resigned, Luther."

"Yeah, they told me. You don't like Kittridge."

"No, I don't."

"He can be neutralized. People up above are going to find out about that NOC list, sooner or later, and when they do, Kittridge ain't going to be giving too many orders."

"Still," Ethan said, "I just don't know why I should want to go back."

"What will you do?"

"Go home. My family has a farm. I know something about that, I think I can help them make it work."

Luther sipped his beer and eyed Ethan. Then he said, "So you'll go back to a simple life."

"Yeah, that's what I'm planning."

"Well, it sounds good," Luther said, trying to be supportive, but not sounding too convinced.

"You don't think it's possible?"

"Young guy like you, anything's possible. Still, I'm not going to pass out from shock if I see you again and you're not wearing overalls."

Ethan laughed.

Luther regarded him silently for a while. "You really liked Jim Phelps, didn't you?"

"I did."

"He is a tough one to figure."

"He was a good guy for a long, long time. Just . . . not long enough." Ethan checked his watch. Time to go. "Gotta catch my flight." He dropped some money on the table, stood and patted Luther on the shoulder. "So, how's it feel being a solid citizen again?"

"Oh, man, I don't know if I can handle it. I'm gonna miss being disreputable."

"If it makes you feel any better," Ethan told him, "I'll always think of you that way."

This was to be his last first-class flight at the IMF's expense. From now on it would be back in the cattle car with the rest of humanity. So Ethan decided he might as well enjoy every minute of it. Slippers, hot towels, French wine, appetizers, choice of entrée, hot fudge sundaes, films, the works. And he knew that he would need all of it just to distract himself from recurring thoughts of Jim, Claire, and his team.

When Ethan informed Kittridge, the day before, that he was resigning from the IMF, Kittridge reacted without emotion. He simply said, "We'll need three or four days, at least, for debriefing."

"There won't be any debriefing," Ethan told him.

Kittridge began to speak, then nodded—the NOC

list debacle pretty much eliminated any leverage that Kittridge held over Ethan.

As the 747 settled into its cruising altitude, Ethan tilted his seat back and sipped a glass of red wine. He hadn't been home in a long time. It would be good to see Mom and Uncle Donald. And who else? No one, really. Working five years with IMF had put him out of touch with anyone except immediate family. Old friends had gone on to other lives. And Ethan's life was not something he could share with any of them.

The isolation of the farm might be just the thing. Hands in the dirt. Of course, it had been Ethan's father who said it would be a shame for the gifted young Ethan Hunt to spend his life on a tractor.

It would be hard to stay home, in truth. It would be hard for him to stay anywhere. And he knew it. Luther Stickell certainly knew it, and that's why he had looked at Ethan so solemnly when Ethan talked about going home to the family farm. He had traveled the world under twenty different identities, he had killed, reluctantly but efficiently, and had nearly been killed on a dozen occasions. He had awakened to the intensity of new mornings that only those people who escape death on a regular basis can understand.

He was going home, but for how long?

A flight attendant began working her way down the aisle, handing out flight folders. When she came to the woman sitting in front of Ethan she smiled, and her eyes jerked quickly to Ethan's face and away. Something about her seemed to change, though Ethan could not identify it.

"Would you like to watch a movie, Miss Walsh?" she said, and the woman accepted one of the folders.

The attendant moved to Ethan. "Would you like to watch a movie, Mr. Hunt?" She smiled coolly.

"No, thank you."

The attendant remained. "Would you consider the cinema of the Caribbean?" she inquired.

He stared at her. Could this be? Was it possible that Kittridge knew him better than he did himself?

She leaned closer. "Aruba, perhaps?"

He froze. And she took his look as an answer in the affirmative.

They had found him. They wanted him back.

The attendant went to get him his cassette, a special cassette that was in a locked case in the cabinet.

Ethan settled back in his seat, knowing that whether he wanted to or not, he was going to watch a movie.

He looked for something in the pockets of his jacket, but did not find what he was looking for. Then he lifted forward the pouch on the back of the seat in front of him. And there, in a red foil wrapper, was a pack of cigarettes. Somehow, he knew they would be there.